What Goes Around Comes Around

When karma is a bitch, can love conquer all?

Ruth Barringham

ISBN: Paperback: 978-0-6454502-2-4
             eBook   978-0-6454502-3-1

Also by Ruth Barringham

Playing For Real
Two Weeks In Corfu
Stand By Me

How to Quit Smoking
How to Write an Article in 15 Minutes
Goodbye Writers Block
7 Day eBook Writing and Publishing System
Living the Laptop Lifestyle
Mission Critical For Life
The Monthly Challenge Writing Series
12 Month Writing Challenge

I dedicate this book to my hardworking husband, Dean, who has helped me through the whole writing process of this book and every other.

Prologue

Karma: What goes around, comes around.

The law of cause and effect.

As you sow, so shall you reap.

Karma can be:

Good
Bad
Individual
Collective

Depending on one's actions, one will reap the fruits of those actions.

Karmic reaction can happen in this life or a future life.

We always accept the good things that happen in our lives, but question the bad things. "Why is this happening to me?"

Chapter 1

*"What goes around, goes around, goes around
Comes all the way back around ~ Justin
Timberlake 2006"*

It was 6pm on a warm, Spring evening and 19 year old Joel Kimball had just finished work for the day.

It was Wednesday so half the week was already over. Three down and two to go.

Joel loved living in Eden, a large coastal town on the Sunshine Coast in Queensland Australia. White sands, plenty of sunshine and so many places he could go and hang out with his friends.

He'd grown up here, so he knew the place well and had plenty of friends, but there were three that were his closest mates, although sometimes he felt annoyed at their lazy attitudes to everything.

But tonight he was happy to meet up with them and hoped that they were as hungry as he was. He fancied a burger, fries, and a big cold drink to wash it all down with.

He walked along with a bit of a spring in his step. It had been a cold winter and was always dark by the time he finished work, but now it was October and the afternoons were staying lighter for longer so he wasn't walking in the dark anymore. Not that he was scared of the dark. He was just sick of always walking around in it.

He could have driven everywhere if he had a car. He had a license but didn't own a car because he couldn't see the point when everywhere he wanted to go was in walking distance and he rarely left town.

He'd had to pass his driving test when he was seventeen in order to be able to do his job.

He worked as an apprentice mechanic for a garage called Hubert Motor Mechanics which was local and walkable from his house. But he needed his driving license so that he could drive the cars around from the back parking lot to the inside workshop to be fixed.

Joel had worked there for almost a year now and worked five, long days a week. He was always grateful that they didn't open on Saturdays. But working long hours every weekday didn't bother him because it meant he earned more money which he was saving so that one day he'd be able to open up a business of his own.

That was his dream. To have his own business because he knew that being the boss wasn't just a better position to be in, but also meant that as the owner, he'd be earning money from the people he employed. Business owners always made far more money than their employees, if they ran the business right, and Joel certainly knew how to do that after working for Hubert's for almost a year and seeing the difference between what high prices they charged for repairs compared to his lowly apprentice wages.

Yep, his boss, Ivan Hubert, certainly knew how to keep the customers happy, keep the money rolling in and how to keep most of it for himself. And that was what Joel planned to do one day too.

His boss, Ivan, wasn't just his boss, he was also his neighbour who lived next door to him. Joel lived with his mother, who was divorced, and his two older siblings had moved out years ago.

As a child, Joel spent hours hanging around the garage watching Ivan and the mechanics working and found it all so fascinating. So, it was no surprise that he eventually ended up working there.

But now, all that was on his mind was food. It was hours since he'd had his lunch and he'd been working flat out all afternoon so he was glad that he was about to meet up with his friends so that he could get something to eat.

He smiled when he thought of his three mates. He called them the Irish Trio because their names were Lachlan, Hamish, and Angus. They weren't Irish at all and were all born and bred right here in Eden, but it was hilarious that they all had Irish names especially considering that their parents were Australian.

Joel and been at school with them and they had all remained friends.

He still liked them, but sometimes he wondered if he'd mentally outgrown them because while Joel had his dream of owning his own business and worked hard all week, his friends were all unemployed and seemed to not want to find a job at all. And as the 3 years went by since leaving school, the Irish Trio seemed to get lazier and lazier till it seemed they couldn't even think of something to do in the evenings.

The problem was that they had never trained for anything and so could only get jobs that paid minimum wages which they always seemed reluctant to do. They'd say things like, 'Why should I work for slave wages?' Joel always thought it amusing that they thought that slaves were paid. But how did they expect to earn more money if they weren't trained in anything?

Over the last few years the Irish Trio each had jobs on and off, just working for local shops and bars, but they kept getting fired for not working hard enough and now it seemed that no one wanted to hire them. So they sat around all day doing nothing much of anything because they had little money so couldn't afford to do much.

None of them had a girlfriend either and didn't even seem capable of attracting any females and none of them had a car. Joel didn't have a car through choice, but the Irish Trio couldn't even afford a car between them.

Joel was now at the main square in town where he'd planned to meet up with his friends and he saw instantly that they were already there, slouching on the wooden benches at a wooden picnic table. They all looked up and gave a slight nod of recognition as Joel approached.

Lachlan was the first to speak. "Finally. We've been waiting ages."

Joel was surprised. "Why? You know what time I finish work so why have you been waiting a long time?"

Hamish cut in before Lachlan could answer. "We were bored so we set off early. Lockie was so useless at playing today that his gaming was as bad as his ugly face."

Joel smiled involuntarily. He didn't want Lachlan to think he was laughing at him, but Hamish was right. Lachlan WAS ugly. When it came to good looks, Lockie missed out completely. Joel sometimes thought he looked like The Hunchback of Notre Dame, but without the hunch. Young girls stared at Lockie and then giggled once he'd passed by. It was sad really, but ugly was ugly and there was nothing Joel could do to change that.

Lachlan was instantly angry with Hamish. "It's just a stupid computer game so what does it matter anyway? We could have played longer but you were just getting pissy about it."

Hamish shrugged off the remark as though he really didn't care. "What have you been up to today Joel, as if I didn't already know."

Joel was used to their teasing him about having a job when they didn't. "Oh, the usual. Out earning money while you three wasted another day playing computer games hour after hour."

It was Angus's turn to speak. "So what? You might earn money, but we don't see you spending much. You're just as broke and bored as us. But at least we spend all day doing what we want to do and not slaving for someone else all day. And at the end of it all, you're no different to us."

"I'm not a dole bludger."

"But you hang out with us, so you're not that great are you?"

"Are you saying you don't want me hanging around with you?"

"No. I'm just saying that you're wasting your time working when you don't have to. None of us has anything to do tonight so we're all the same except we've been having fun all day while you've been working."

The other two were nodding in agreement.

Joel was unimpressed. He didn't care what they thought because he knew he was working towards having a future while their future was to be doing exactly what they were doing now, with no money and no ambition. He simply shrugged.

Lachlan moaned, "It's so boring around here. Every night there's nothing to do. This town sucks."

Joel sighed. "It's your choice to be bored. There's plenty to do around here. There's cafes, pubs, the beach, plenty of shops. The problem is that you guys never have any money to do anything. And if you had a job, you'd appreciate the nights more because you'd be able to enjoy it. But you do nothing all day and then have nothing to do all night either. I don't care about having not much to do because I've been busy all day, so doing nothing is a nice change. But for you it's the norm.

"I know someone who's in hospital and he's been stuck there for weeks and all he talks about is how great it would be to be able to walk around outside for a change. You can do that now so you're better off than someone stuck in hospital."

"Yeah, well, at least if you're stuck in hospital you know that the boredom will end one day. Ours won't." Lachlan folded his arms across his chest petulantly.

Joel decided to change the subject. "I'm hungry. I fancy burger and chips. How about you guys?"

The other three looked down at the ground as though they didn't want to answer.

"Can't afford it," said Lachlan.

"Me neither," said Hamish.

Angus just shrugged.

There was a few minutes of silence. Joel wanted to go and get something to eat but he didn't want to pay for the others. He never wanted to fall into the trap of always being the one who pays or everything. So he never shouted them a free anything.

Angus slowly looked up and said, "You know, we don't have to pay for food."

The other two smiled and nodded but Joel was confused and asked, "You know where there's free food?"

"Yeah," said Angus with a knowing grin. "You just have to know how not to pay for it."

"What do you mean?"

Lachlan grinning at Joel. "These shops make plenty of money, so they don't miss much when people don't pay for things. In fact, I've been told that they factor in theft as part of their pricing."

Joel was shocked. "You mean you want to STEAL burger and fries? You know they make you pay when you order, right?"

The Irish Trio smiled at each other knowingly. Then Hamish looked at Joel. "Not fast food. Just groceries. There's that store around the corner that's always busy at night. If we time it right, we can take whatever we want, and they won't even know."

"How do you know?" asked Joel.

"We've done it before," said Angus and snorted a laugh.

"When?"

"Lots of times. And not just that place. If you wait till they're not looking, you can get free stuff from just about anywhere."

Joel had never heard them talk about this before. "You mean you go around nicking stuff all the time?"

"Yep," said Lachlan. "If the government won't give us enough money to buy stuff, then it's their fault that things get stolen."

Joel couldn't believe what he was hearing. "You mean the government is making you steal stuff?"

"Exactly," said Lachlan proudly, missing the sarcasm in Joel's voice. "Come with us and we'll show you."

"You want me to steal stuff too?"

"Yeah, why? Think you're too good for us all of a sudden?"

Joel smiled, "No, it's not sudden at all."

Lachlan still missed the sarcasm. "Just come with us and watch what we do. You don't have to do anything if you're scared."

"I'm not scared, I just don't want to. I can afford to pay for my food."

Hamish chimed in almost begging Joel to go with them. "You'll enjoy it. It's like watching the masters of free stuff doing their thing. You won't believe how much you can get away with when the staff are too stupid to see what's going on. Just come and watch."

The Irish Trio begged and taunted Joel until he gave in. "All right, all right. I'll come with you. But don't be surprised if I act like I don't know you once we get in there."

And that was all they needed to hear. The other three stood up and made their way to the nearby grocery store, while Joel followed reluctantly. He had a bad feeling about what they were about to do.

Within minutes they were stood outside the store. They all looked through the window. Lachlan told Joel what they had to do. "First, we check out the layout of the store and where the staff are and what they're doing. See, when you look you can see that there are four people working in there and lots of customers. It's pretty busy for a small place.

"Three of them are serving at the counter. The other is talking to a customer in one of the back aisles. That's good because they're all distracted.

"So, what we'll do is go in and walk around and see what we want to get and then decide how we're going to do it and when. Just keep your head down so that they can't see our faces on the security cameras.

"Don't worry Joel. It'll be fine. Nothing will go wrong. You'll see."

But Joel didn't feel confident at all.

Chapter 2

Joel didn't feel like the so-called 'plan' for stealing food was good. In fact, any plan for stealing anything was bad. He'd never seen the point of theft, especially for small items like groceries. If you got caught, you'd get a criminal record, so why risk it for so little? If he was going to steal anything it would be a million dollar heist of some sort so that it would be life-changing, not just pinching items that were only worth a few dollars. It just seemed so stupid.

Not only that, he had his reputation to think of. He worked locally and knew so many local people. He didn't ever want them to know him as a thief, especially as he wanted to own his own business here one day.

But he felt obligated to go along with his friends because they seemed so adamant that they knew what they were doing and said that they'd done it so many times before and had never been caught.

Once inside the store, they walked up and down every aisle and he could see that the other three were taking a mental note of all the people that were in there.

After they'd traversed every aisle, they walked up and down them all again.

Lachlan eventually spoke. "There are customers in every single aisle and as some leave, someone new walks in roughly every 15 seconds. And whenever the staff aren't serving customers, they start stacking shelves so they're busy all the time, which is good."

Joel was amazed at Lockie's surveillance skills and felt he'd missed his calling in the police or with a security firm.

"So, what next?" asked Joel.

Lachlan spoke to him quietly while casually looking at items on a shelf in an attempt to make it look like he either wasn't speaking to him, or he was only talking about the cans food he was looking at. "We wait till it's quiet so that there aren't as many people here. We don't want too many witnesses. We also don't want anyone getting in our way when we exit."

"What are we going to get?" asked Angus, looking at the floor as he spoke.

Lachlan picked up a couple of cans and started turning them over in his hands as though he was interested in them. "We need to get whatever doesn't need a can opener and doesn't need cooking. So, I reckon it's either chocolate or salads because there's some pretty nice looking ready-made ones in the chiller and they even come with a plastic fork. Or we go for sandwiches which are also in the chiller."

"I say go for the sandwiches," said Hamish. "The chiller is near the door on the left. The counter is in the middle of the store to the right. We can grab at least two sandwiches each so we'll have eight altogether, and we can make it out the door before the staff have a chance to get out from behind the counter and chase us.

"Problem is though, when they're not serving customers, they're stacking shelves, so we need to time it so that even though there are still customers being served, there's not enough of them to get in our way or get a good look at us."

"Eight sandwiches?" asked Joel. "I said I'd come along and watch. I don't want to do it."

"Oh, for God's sake, Joel. Man up and grow a pair," said Lachlan. "Once you came in here with us, you were in it with us. You can't just stand there like a douche while we run out of here. Everyone knows we're all together. We've been in here walking around for ages so whether you help us or not, you'll be just as guilty as us so you may as well just do it."

Joel didn't know what to say. He didn't want to steal any sandwiches, but Lachlan was right. He'd come in with them and had stayed with them, so he looked just as guilty as them no matter what he did. He felt trapped and helpless, and his only hope was that they were right about never getting caught.

Joel's lack of response was taken as acceptance.

"Here's what we'll do. We'll split up. But not too much. Stay together, but not too together. We'll make our way slowly back up to the chiller and when the time's right, I'll give you the word and we call grab and go. Got it?"

The other two nodded, but Joel was unsure. He was unsure of what he was supposed to do and unsure that he wanted to do it at all. In fact, he didn't want to do it but now he felt he had no choice. And again, his silence was taken as acceptance.

"Right. Go." At Lachlan's command the other two took a few steps away, and acting as casually as they could, the three began their nonchalant walk to the front of the store. Joel followed closely behind, but felt almost sick at the thought of what they were about to do.

The customer number had gone down and although there were one or two still in each aisle, most of them were at the counter being served or waiting to be served.

And then the timing was suddenly right when most of the customers were served and had left the store and no others came in. That only left about six other people still in the aisles and none at the front of the store.

At the same time the four would-be thieves began to look in the chiller, trying to look as though they were interested in purchasing a cold drink or a tightly sealed salad in a bowl. Three of them kept flicking quick glances behind them while the fourth one kept his head down with a frown on his face and an increased beating of his heart. None of them spoke.

As the door swung shut behind the last exiting customer, the Irish Trio simultaneously reached their hands towards the chiller, grabbed a sealed sandwich in each hand and bolted for the door.

Joel, never having done this before, was a couple of beats behind them so that by the time he realised what was going on, he only managed to grab one sandwich and as he turned he saw that the first of the Irish Trio was already out the door.

With his heart literally pounding in his chest he headed for the door in a fast walk because he couldn't seem to bring himself to run.

Before he reached the door it swung shut behind the third exiting thief who disappeared into the night without breaking stride.

He reached out to pull open the door with his sandwich-less hand, but even as he did so he had the sinking feeling that he wasn't going to escape.

Chapter 3

Joel had been right about the front door of the store not opening for him. He'd learnt a simple lesson the hard way that night, and that was that the door could be locked electronically by the staff pressing a button under the counter across the room.

He'd had to stay at the store for quite some time before he was able to leave. His friends (or his so-called friends) who'd left him behind had kept texting him to ask where he was, but he hadn't answered them.

Now he was walking home on his own, angry and humiliated at what had happened.

When the door hadn't opened, Joel knew he was in trouble. One of the staff, a guy who looked about 30-something with long, wavy hair, had walked up to him and had calmly given him an option. Joel could either stay there while he called the police, or go with him to a back room where they could talk.

Walking though the store with all the staff and customers staring had been embarrassing, but it was better than being arrested.

The guy had taken him to a small staff room where Joel had displayed a small act of defiance and squeezed the plastic-wrapped sandwich (which he'd forgotten about until then) and thrown it on the table, stating that the sandwich was still on the premises so technically he hadn't stolen anything.

But the guy no longer seemed concerned about the thefts that had occurred. Instead, he calmly introduced himself as Algar and said that he was the evening store manager. Joel thought what a stupid hippy name that was.

Algar sat across the table from Joel, the squashed sandwich ever-present between them, and said that he thought Joel had not wanted to steal anything and that he'd looked as though he'd been pressured into doing so.

Joel thought that was remarkably perceptive of him, but he still just wanted the guy to stop talking so that he could leave because he knew that the guy was just going to lecture him about how wrong it was to steal stuff. But instead, he said something totally weird and unexpected.

He asked Joel if he'd heard about karma. Joel tried not to show his surprise at such a strange question and only shrugged in response.

Algar then went into a long explanation about karma and how it works. He said that nothing physical or emotional ever happens in isolation and that every action and reaction has an affect and he even talked about a hummingbird flapping its wings in America causing a typhoon in Japan.

He also talked about how negative actions can go full circle and create an even bigger negative reaction. He said that Joel's actions had created his own bad karma which would eventually travel full circle and back to him and so he would have to watch out for a chain reaction of negative events that could swing around and hurt him in the end.

Joel smirked and snorted at the warning, but Algar seemed serious and didn't see anything funny about it. He told Joel that as long as he heeded the warning, he may be okay. But if he didn't, then he might not see the negative events coming and may suffer.

Joel thought about it all the way home. The guy, Algar, had likened the attempted theft of the sandwich to the hummingbird flapping its wings and he told Joel to be careful that he didn't get swept away by the resulting typhoon.

As he reached home and put his key in the front door lock, he decided to forget about all the ramblings he'd been forced to listen to about karma.

But at the same time, he couldn't stop thinking about it.

Chapter 4

Joel reached out his hand and silenced his alarm clock and immediately sat up, threw back the covers and swung his feet to the floor.

He stretched his arms high above his head and yawned at the same time. As he engaged his mind he thought, 'What day is it? Oh yeah, it's Thursday.' And then he remembered the strange happenings of the night before.

He'd texted his friend Lachlan on the way home and told him he was going straight home and that next time they wanted to do something stupid, to leave him out of it. He had no intention of ever doing that again or telling them what had happened.

He stood up and opened his bedroom curtains. It was a warm, sunny day with not a cloud in the sky.

He ran his fingers through his brown, wavy hair as he walked to the bathroom and thought about the karma warning. It was such a bright day that it didn't feel as though anything bad could happen, and he thought to himself, 'Maybe I should just be a bit more careful about crossing the road for the next few days.' Then he laughed at himself for even caring.

As soon as he was washed, dressed and his bed was made, he headed downstairs, promising himself that he wouldn't tell his mother about what happened last night. He knew she wouldn't be angry with him, but she would be upset, and he never liked to upset his mother. Her disappointment always seemed worse than her anger.

When he entered the kitchen she was making herself some toast. She looked up and greeted him, asked if he wanted toast too and put two more slices in the toaster.

As they ate and drank coffee together his mother chatted happily about Joel's older siblings.

Joel and his mother, Olivia Kimball, were quite happy living together. She worked at home as a computer programmer. She loved her work and when she wasn't busy doing it, she was immersed in reading the latest book on programming.

Joel's parents had divorced when he was young, and he hadn't seen his father for years and didn't even know where he lived any more.

Olivia's job had always made her financially independent and she seemed to have no interest in remarrying, but she did have quite an active social life and plenty of friends.

His sister, Raelene Kimball, was twenty two, three years older than Joel, and had moved out a few months ago and now rented an apartment above one of the stores in town. She worked at the local supermarket and had ambitions to be the store manager one day.

His older brother, Morgan Kimball, was twenty five, was engaged, but lived alone in a small rented house. He was an electrician who worked for himself and always had plenty of local work, mostly working for the local builders. Sometimes he worked for Owen Hubert who was also a builder and the son of Joel's boss and neighbour, Ivan Hubert.

Joel's mother was telling him that Raelene was working more hours every day so that she could learn more about the running of the store. "You know Joel, one of her regular customers asked her out but she turned him down because she says she doesn't have time for dating. But I think she's just not interested. She just seems so disinterested in the whole dating and having a boyfriend thing. But I suppose it's a good thing in a way. Maybe she's waiting for Mr. Right but how will she know if she turns down every offer of a date?"

Joel smiled as she talked. He'd heard her ask this same question about Raelene many times before, and it was as if she was asking herself.

Without pausing she then went on to tell Joel about his brother too. "Morgan has so much work on lately that he's the opposite of Raelene. She has time to date but doesn't want to while Morgan wants to go out on dates with his fiancé, but doesn't have the time. He's even had to work all last weekend. I hope he doesn't have to work this weekend too or he's going to be exhausted. You know he can only burn the candle at both ends for a short time before he burns out."

Joel smiled again at another thing that his mother said often about Morgan working too hard. But he was glad that she had so much to say so that she didn't ask him where he went last night. He just hoped that there was no one in the store last night who knew his mother, but he hadn't recognised anyone.

After he and his mother finished breakfast, he packed his lunch and set off to work. He only lived a short distance from the garage so the walk there took him less than 20 minutes.

When he arrived the two other mechanics, Ken and Joe, were already there but his boss, Ivan, was absent which was unusual. 'No Ivan yet?' he asked, helping himself to a cup of coffee from the drip machine and sitting down with Ken and Joe.

Ken was the older of the three of them and Joel figured he must be in his fifties. Ken's body shape was what Joel's mother referred to as 'portly' and he had a full head of silver hair. Ken had worked there for over twenty years and had a spare set of keys so Joel figured he must have been the one who opened that morning.

The other mechanic, Joe, was about thirty years younger than Ken, still in his twenties and had apprenticed there years ago after the previous mechanic had retired. Joe was single and still lived at home with his mother and every day would go to the pub for his dinner and a few beers which partly explained why he couldn't afford a place of his own.

Joel wished that Joe had a different name because it was too much like his own and when someone called out to either of them, they'd both look round, unsure which one had been called.

Ken took a long swig from his coffee mug and said, "No, it's weird. No sign of Ivan at all and he didn't mention being late yesterday before we left. I don't think I've ever known him to be late."

He then changed the subject and talked about all the jobs they had to do that day. It was a busy garage. Already several more cars had been parked out in the back car park this morning and the owners had put their keys in the safety box and gone, which was the usual practice for cars that had been booked in and their owner's had to get to work.

"Joel, you carry on with the car from yesterday. Joe, you bring the first car in from out back and get it up on the lift.

That way we can make a start and when Ivan gets here he can tell us if he wants us working on something else."

The three men finished their coffee, put their cups in the sink, put on their overalls, and went out onto the workshop floor. Joel started working on the car he hadn't finished yesterday, and Joe went into the office to see which car was first in line. Ken opened the front roller doors and sunlight flooded in.

They all carried on working for an hour, still wondering what had happened to Ivan. Ken kept taking phone calls from customers and writing the jobs in the workbook. But when the phone rang again it wasn't a customer. It was Ivan. They could tell because Ken said, "Finally! We were beginning to think you'd been abducted by aliens. What's going on?" As Ken listened, the smile slowly faded from his face and he began to interject what he was hearing with, "You're kidding. Are you serious? No! It can't be true." He turned away from the other two and went into the office and shut the door, still listening as he went.

Joel and Joe exchanged puzzled looks and went back to work, all the time glancing through the window of the office door, where they could see Ken sitting at the desk, looking down with his fingertips on his forehead, shaking his head and speaking low and seriously with Ivan.

After a few minutes Joe came up to Joel and they both stood staring through the window. "What do you reckon?"

Joel had no idea. "I reckon he's talking to Ivan but other than that..."

"No doubt we'll find out, but it doesn't look good. Look out. Here he comes."

Ken had put down the phone, sighed deeply, and came back into the workshop. "We're going to close for lunch at twelve."

Joe asked, "Why? We never close for lunch. What's going on? Where's Ivan? Is he alright?"

Ken put up a calming hand. "Ivan's okay but it's a long story. I don't want to tell you out here. We'll close at twelve." And with that he walked away and went back to work.

Joe shrugged at Joel who shook his head, and they went back to work too with none of them saying a word to each other. It felt tense.

Promptly at twelve o'clock, Ken lowered the front roller doors and went outside with a sign he'd made with a thick marker pen and a piece of copy paper that said, 'Open At 1pm' and he taped it on the front of the doors. Joel was surprised because they usually only took a forty five minute lunch break each which were staggered so they never closed, or took an hour off.

In the small kitchen, they made another pot of coffee and all sat round the small lunch table.

"Ivan won't be back for a while and asked me to look after the place while he's gone," Ken told them.

"For how long?" Asked Joel.

"No idea. Probably a few weeks at least." Ken leaned on the table and took on a more serious tone. "Look, something terrible happened last night. Ivan's daughter, Nadine, was visiting him and after she left, she was hit by a drunk driver and killed. Ivan's spent all night with the police and with Nadine's husband, Owen."

Joe and Joel sat in silence waiting to hear more.

"The worst part is that Ivan seems to be blaming himself. He felt ill last night. Nadine was worried about getting sick too and because she's so close to having the baby now, two months according to Ivan, she thought it best to leave.

"But he was too ill to drive her, and she said she wouldn't get in the car with him anyway, so she walked. Poor thing didn't have a chance because the driver mounted the curb at speed and hit her from behind, so she and the baby were killed instantly. Apparently, and I shouldn't really repeat this, she was struck so hard that she travelled twenty metres through the air.

"The police contacted Owen first who had to go and identify the body and then he called Ivan."

"Has the guy been arrested?" asked Joel.

"Yeah. He's initially being charged with reckless driving, drink driving and vehicular manslaughter but hopefully they think of more things to charge him with. Ivan said the police were disgusted with the drunken state he was in, and they said that because Nadine was so far along in her pregnancy that they'll probably charge him with two deaths. But that doesn't help Ivan right now."

There was a brief silence, none of them knew what to say. Then Joel asked, "He didn't have any other children, did he?"

"No," said Ken. "His wife couldn't have any more children after Nadine was born and she had to have a complete hysterectomy. Nadine was never happy being an only child so when she married Owen she said she wanted to have at least six kids, probably more. But now look. Only twenty five years old and she's gone."

Joe sat back in his chair, slapped his hands on the thighs and said, "How can anyone be so unfortunate? It's like Ivan is plagued by death and drunk drivers."

He was talking about Ivan's wife who had been killed by a drunk driver just over two years before that. He and Ken had both worked for Ivan during that unfortunate event and it had been two months before Ivan came back to work that time. They wondered if it would be longer this time.

Joel had only been there for just under a year, so he wasn't around when it happened. But because Ivan was his neighbour, he had still been a part of the tragedy when it happened and had attended the funeral along with his mother and Raelene and Morgan. Her death had been so unexpected that it shocked everyone for a long time.

And now another drunk driver had taken his daughter and unborn grandchild. What were the chances of that?

Briefly he thought about the previous evening of sandwich thievery and Algar's warning of bad Karma, a chain reaction of negative events and an eventual typhoon that would sweep Joel away.

But clearly, he was wrong. These may be negative events, but it didn't happen to Joel personally or a member of his own family.

Instead, it happened again to poor Ivan.

So that couldn't be Joel's fault.

Could it?

Chapter 5

Ken, Joe and Joel sat in the lunch room for what seemed like a long time, talking about how happy Ivan had been at the thought of not only being a grandfather, but eventually being the grandfather of at least six grandchildren that Nadine had planned. It was just what he needed after losing his wife two years ago.

When he'd returned back to work, he'd acted as though nothing was different. He never mentioned his wife and didn't allow others to either. But apart from that he'd just acted like his usual self.

But this time it was different.

Losing Nadine and the baby was going to be harder for him to recover from.

The conversation in the lunchroom drifted from Ivan to the garage and the running of it.

They ate their lunch while they discussed details of what they were going to do.

Ken said that he'd take care of the paperwork, of booking in jobs, and would make sure that he took on less work now that there were only three of them for the foreseeable future. But they all agreed that if necessary, they'd all work overtime to keep the place going until Ivan returned.

Then they discussed what to do about Ivan and quickly agreed that they'd close on time and visit him at home.

"Are we going to walk there?" asked Joel.

"No, we'll go in my car," said Ken. "That way I can drive home. Joel you'll already be home, and Joe, you can walk to the pub from there. No doubt you'll be fine-dining there as usual."

Joe smiled at Ken's sarcasm. "It might not be fine, but it's filling, and I can watch TV, read the paper, and relax and unwind there."

"What are we going to say to him?" asked Joel. He wasn't looking forward to going even though he knew they had to.

"We'll play it by ear," said Ken. "Goodness knows what it will be like. Ivan was crying on the phone earlier. He's pretty messed up about this. When his missus died he was mostly quiet, but this time it seems to be the opposite. He was yelling and crying and even though I couldn't see him, I knew that snot was streaming from his nose. He seems to have completely lost his composure and doesn't give a shit about it."

"I guess he's got a lot more on his mind," said Joe. "Geez, I can't believe this has happened. It just doesn't seem real. You know, you hear about people dying all the time and you think that yeah, it's a shame, but that's all. But when it happens to someone you know, it's like "POW." It hits you hard, like being punched."

Joel knew exactly what he meant, even though it was impossible to put into words.

After lunch, which was mostly a silent affair after that, they re-opened the garage, each of them dreading the next few hours because it suddenly felt so strange. So different.

Joel hadn't been back at work very long when his phone rang. He wiped his hands on a rag and took out his phone. It was Lachlan calling. He went to the back car park as he answered.

Lachlan was with Angus and Hamish, and he had Joel on speaker. "What do you want?" Joel had always told them not to call or text him when he was working so he was annoyed at the call, even more so after hearing about Nadine.

"Is it true? Was your boss's daughter killed? We've heard the rumours but couldn't believe it. So, what happened?"

Joel was instantly furious with Lachlan's callousness, and he snapped "how the hell should I know? I don't even know what rumours you heard. And don't you think it's a bit insensitive calling me for gruesome details? I did know her you know."

Hamish chimed in next. "Oh come on, Joel. If anyone knows what's going on it's you. You work for the guy so you MUST know."

Joel struggled to keep his voice down. "Don't you three clowns ever think of anyone but yourselves? Do you have any idea what it's like for us here? We have to deal with it face to face and speak to Ivan and he's absolutely gutted."

Lachlan ignored Joel's plea for mercy. "Oh, stop being such a drama queen. He's your boss not your friend. We're your friends and we're just trying to find out the truth about what happened."

"I don't know exactly what happened," he lied. "Ivan's not even here today. We're going to see him later after work. And speaking of which, we're rushed off our feet without Ivan here, so I have to go.' He ended the call before they could say anymore."

The news about Nadine's death and Ivan's breakdown had upset him more than he thought it would and at the moment the whole thing had a surreal feeling about it as though it all couldn't be true.

He put his phone in his locker so that if it rang again he wouldn't hear it and went back to work, still annoyed at his friends' tactlessness.

But the call wasn't the end of tactless questioning. Customers kept pouring in for the rest of the afternoon asking if it was true about Ivan's daughter and wanting to know details. The three mechanics were taken aback by the continuous visitors and all their questions, and without saying a word to each other they all began acting busier than they actually were to try and dodge questions.

They had their heads under car bonnets, worked under cars, worked with the service machines and drove cars in and out of the workshop, all the time avoiding questions.

And if that wasn't hard enough to deal with, the phone seemed to constantly ring with customers asking questions too. So, after an hour of phone interruptions, Ken told the others that they were no longer taking calls for the rest of the day and he unplugged the base unit of the phone.

Joe asked about legitimate calls that would be missed but Ken said that not one of them was a legitimate call and that anyone needing their car fixed would call back tomorrow.

At three thirty, Joel went to the kitchen to take a break. He took his phone out of his locker and checked to see if he'd any missed calls from his thoughtless mates. There were no more calls from them, but he had missed a call from his mother. He called her back.

"Joel are you okay? It's terrible about what happened to poor Nadine. Is everything okay there?"

Joel smiled at his mother's concern for him. "Yeah, I'm fine but it's been a terrible afternoon with people coming in and phoning to ask about what's happened"

"I can imagine. It's all everyone's talking about. This morning I had no idea what had happened. It seems the local gossip was a bit slow about catching up with this tragedy."

"Same here. There was no mention of it from anyone. But this afternoon we've even had to unplug the phone to stop people calling and asking about it."

"I'm not surprised. I'm so shook up by the news that I can't seem to concentrate and get any work done. Poor Ivan."

Joel could tell that his mother was crying. "Yeah, I know. We're going to see him after work but to be honest I'm not looking forward to it."

"I don't blame you. I don't think he's come out of shock yet."

"Have you seen him?"

"Of course. I went round as soon as I heard the news. Nadine's husband Owen was there too. I think both of them have been up all night"

"Oh God. Poor Owen. What did they say?"

"Not much. They both looked and sounded exhausted. A few others visited while I was there and so many others have been visiting since. It's like a nightmare. I wanted to be there, hoping I could help but what can you say or do when something like this happens?"

"He's already lost his wife just two years ago and now a drunk driver kills his daughter and unborn grandchild. And poor Owen. Oh Joel, this whole thing is devastating, and it makes me feel helpless."

"I know what you mean. I have no idea what to say when I see him or how long we'll be there. Ken's driving us there straight after work, so I won't be home for dinner. I'll just get myself something later."

Olivia Kimball started crying again. "Oh, that's fine. I don't think I want to cook anyway. Eating is the last thing on my mind right now."

Joel felt sad for his mother. "Look, try not to feel too bad. I have to go now. I'm just on my break and I have to get back to work. I'll be home after I've been to see Ivan."

"Oh Joel. I'm sorry."

"Don't be. This is a crazy thing and everyone's upset. It just blows my mind every time I think about it."

"What's going to happen with the garage?"

"Oh, we're going to keep the place running, but that's all we know for now."

"That's good. I'll let you go and get back to work. I'll see you when I see you."

"Okay. Bye Mum."

"Bye sweetheart." And they both ended the call.

Joel put his phone back in his locker and thought about how weird this whole thing was. It almost felt surreal as if it wasn't true and any minute Ivan would walk into the workshop, apologise for being late and then everything would go back to normal.

But that wasn't going to happen. Nadine and her unborn child had been hit and killed by a drunk driver last night, and nothing could undo that.

Last night was also the night that Joel had been caught stealing a sandwich which was another thing that couldn't be undone, no matter how much he wished it could.

38

The whole thing had been humiliating and he just hoped his mother would never find out because she would be so hurt and disappointed that he'd do such a stupid and dishonest thing. He should never have listened to his stupid friends. Why the hell did he let them talk him into it?

And then to top it all off he'd had to sit and listen to the hippy manager telling him that stealing the sandwich, which technically he hadn't stolen because he never left the shop with it, but he did destroy it, had caused bad karma which would cause a chain reaction of bad events. What garbage.

But, he had to admit, terrible things had happened shortly after that. In fact, it was terrible what happened, but it hadn't happened to Joel himself, although it did have a knock-on effect that had negatively impacted his life.

But all that being caused by a sandwich? That, he couldn't believe.

Or at least that's what he told himself as he headed back to work with the feeling of The Sword of Damocles hanging over his head.

Chapter 6

After the three mechanics closed up the shop for the day, they headed off to see Ivan with nothing being said in the car during the short journey. As they got out of the car in front of Ivan's house, their collective intake of nervous breath was almost audible. All of them wanted to be there to support their grieving boss, yet at the same time they dreaded going in.

As they walked to the door Joel said, "What are we going to say?"

"How the hell should I know?" said Ken as he knocked on the door. Without waiting for an answer, he opened the door and the three of them went inside, closing the door silently behind them.

Joel noticed immediately that the house smelled musty, like sweat, even though the air conditioning was on. Maybe it was because of all the people that his mother said had been going in and out all day.

But there was no one there now. Ivan and his son-in-law Owen Johnson were alone in the open-plan part of the house, sitting at the dining table. They weren't speaking and didn't even look up when the others entered.

Ken, Joe and Joel exchanged quick glances with each other that said, 'Now what do we do?'

Ken spoke first. "Ivan I'm so sorry." There was no response from Ivan, so he carried on. "I wanted to come and give you words of wisdom, but I really don't know what to say. This whole thing is so incomprehensible."

Suddenly Ivan burst into tears and cried audibly, putting his hands over his face, his shoulders convulsing as he sobbed.

Owen didn't react at all. He just stared into space as he had been doing the whole time. He seemed numb.

Again, the three mechanics shared a helpless glance at each other.

Ken turned and moved towards the electric kettle sitting on the kitchen countertop close by. "I'll make tea."

As he busied himself, Joe sat down at the table and Joel, not knowing what else to do, sat down too. No one spoke for a while, but Ivan's sobbing abated when the cups of tea were placed on the table. Ken sat down too.

Ivan picked up his cup immediately and sipped his tea, even though it must have been too hot. Then he started to speak and told them how Nadine had come to visit him the previous evening, but he hadn't been feeling well.

"She stopped driving because she's so close to giving birth that it's hard for her to fit behind the wheel. So, she walks everywhere.

"I normally would have driven her home, but it was the darnedest thing. I'd stayed back a bit to finish some paperwork after you guys left, and on the way home I stopped off to get a sandwich for dinner from that late night store a couple of streets away from work. You know, the one that has that weird hippy manager in the evenings with a name like Agar or Algar or something."

41

The mere mention of that store and Algar and sandwiches made Joel's stomach jolt. He hoped his shock wasn't visible and sipped his tea nervously. Ivan must have been there shortly after Joel and his stolen sandwich incident. He just hoped Ivan hadn't seen him leaving from the back room, but with what else had happened that night, he doubted Ivan would even care. But it didn't stop him from feeling guilty.

Ivan went on. "I bought an egg mayo sandwich and there must have been something wrong with it because after I ate it, I had a shower and then Nadine turned up. I wasn't even expecting her, but I'm always glad to see her." Tears welled up in his eyes and quickly poured down his face as he carried on.

"But within half an hour my stomach felt weird and soon I was on the toilet with diarrhea like I've never seen before. And every time I got off the toilet, I was straight back on there again within ten minutes.

"So that's why Nadine walked home, because I'd eaten that rotten egg sandwich. Why the hell didn't I leave the damn thing till after my shower, then with Nadine showing up I probably wouldn't have eaten it till she'd gone. Or maybe not eaten the damn thing at all, and she'd still be alive.

"I should have just driven her home anyway. Shitting my pants in the car would have been preferable to this!" And with that he began a fresh bout of crying, pulling a handkerchief out of his pocket and blowing his nose loudly.

They could tell he'd been crying a lot because his face was so red and puffy with deep, dark circles under his eyes.

Nadine's husband Owen, who had been sitting in silence the whole time looked at Ivan and put a comforting hand on his shoulder.

Ivan returned the handkerchief to his pocket and continued. "She didn't even see the car coming. She was walking on the footpath where she was supposed to be. It was narrow with a stone wall at the side."

Ivan paused as a quick bout of tears got the better of him. He recovered fast and carried on. "They say she died instantly, couldn't have gotten out of the way even if she'd seen it coming. The driver was so drunk and was going so fast that he hit the curb and mounted the footpath behind her. She didn't stand a chance."

A fresh bout of tears interrupted him again. The three mechanics picked up their cups and sipped their tea almost in unison, not knowing what else to do or say.

Ivan made use of his handkerchief again. "When Owen came over last night I thought he was going to tell me that Nadine had gone into early labour. I couldn't believe what he'd actually come to say.

"I prayed that it wasn't true. It just had to be some kind of mistake and that Nadine and the baby were fine. I just didn't want to believe it. I felt even more ill than I did from eating that rotten sandwich and I'd have thrown up if there'd been anything left in my stomach." Another loud batch of tears stopped him from saying anything else.

Owen took over. "I was surprised when I saw the police at my door and by all accounts they arrived soon after the accident.

"You know, they're extremely tactful when they have to tell you something like that, but it didn't make the news less devastating."

Owen, like Ivan, looked as though he'd been crying a lot, but Owen seemed more depressed than tearful now. "And it was just like Ivan said, I was listening to what they were telling me but I was hoping that they were mistaken and it wasn't true. It was like I was actually praying that they were wrong.

"They drove me to the scene of the accident so that I could make a positive I.D. I didn't have to do it straight away, but I wanted to. I needed to see.

"Nadine was already in an ambulance, covered by a sheet. They said her face was unrecognisable because she'd slammed face-first into the ground. But I knew it was her clothes and her handbag." Owen's eyes filled with tears and Ivan spoke again.

"The police came here later and talked and talked to us. They seemed to think that Nadine might have somehow known the drunk driver and that it was murder. They wanted to know where she'd been all day and why she was walking alone.

"I told them that the whole thing happened because of that rotten sandwich." He looked heavenwards and said pleadingly, "Why am I being punished? What did I ever do wrong? I lost my wife and now my daughter and my unborn grandchild and all the grandchildren I could have had." His tears flowed once more.

Joel was uncomfortable. He hated being a part of all this sadness, but he could tell that Ivan needed to talk so he sat quietly and sipped his tea.

Ivan blew his nose. "Owen and I have a funeral to sort out now. It has to be done. But this is it. My life will never be normal again. No father ever expects to bury his child." He paused for a few seconds and the silence felt heavy with no one knowing what to say.

Ivan looked at his three mechanics. "I suppose you want to know what's happening at the garage. Well, I don't know and right now, I don't care. I don't give a damn. Maybe things will be different after the funeral, but right now work is the last thing on my mind, so you'll have to manage on your own."

Ken assured him that he needn't worry about the business because he would take care of everything. But Ivan didn't even look up and seemed as though he'd already stopped listening.

* * *

The following week seemed to fly by for Joel. At work they were extremely busy without Ivan there but that was a good thing because it stopped him thinking too much about what had happened. A small part of his mind still couldn't believe it was true.

At home it seemed no less busy because neighbours kept calling round to discuss how Ivan was doing and, it seemed, that they always wanted to know what Joel knew about it. They didn't seem to understand that Joel wasn't in contact with Ivan because he wasn't at work.

He also felt sorry for his mother who was grieving because she'd known Nadine quite well. His brother and sister, Morgan and Raelene, kept visiting every day too, so their house always seemed to be full of people.

But it wasn't just the non-stop visitors that made Joel's life so busy, it was also because he'd started helping out his mother more by doing the dishes and bringing in the washing and other small jobs. It was as if he had a whole new appreciation of having his mother in his life after experiencing how swiftly Ivan had lost his daughter. Sudden death could happen to anyone, so it felt important to have gratitude for those people still in his life, especially his mother who he'd always been close to both physically and emotionally.

* * *

The funeral was on the following Friday. The crematorium was so full that many people had to listen to the service through speakers outside.

Joel was immediately saddened when he walked in and saw the tiny coffin next to the large one. It was clearly a double ceremony for Nadine and her baby.

He sat with his family in a large group with the other mechanics and their families and Ivan and Owen and their families.

When everyone was seated a woman behind a podium began to speak. As she did so, photos of Nadine began to parade one by one across a large screen above the coffins.

Ivan and Owen immediately burst into tears and despite his resolve to be strong, so did Joel, along with everyone else in the room. He looked down because he didn't want to see any more photos. He didn't want to be there at all. Funerals were so depressing.

After it was over and everyone had said their goodbyes to each other, Joel wanted to go home. His mother however, insisted that he attend the gathering afterwards that was being held in a large function room upstairs at the local pub.

He wanted to say no but his mother was so upset already so he said yes and spent the time standing on his own, nursing just one schooner of beer and trying to avoid talking to anyone, or only those talking about things other than the accident or the funeral. As soon as they broached those subjects he'd walk away.

Afterwards, his mother wanted them to go out for dinner with Raelene and Morgan, a family meal, but Joel didn't want to go and said that it had been a stressful day and he just wanted to go home. His mother said okay and hugged him goodbye. He set off walking home, ready to let the fresh air lift his mood.

And he did feel better, but not back to normal. It all still felt so strange that Nadine was gone and he wondered what it would be like working with Ivan again if he ever came back to work. Previously, Ivan had talked a lot about his first grandchild who was soon to be born and he was really excited about it. Maybe he'd asked Ken and Joe what things were like at work when Ivan returned after the death of his wife. What did they say to him? What subjects were taboo?

"Joel!"

He looked around and saw his three friends approaching. "What are you so dressed up for?" asked Lachlan, flipping up the end of Joel's tie.

"I've been to the funeral."

"Oh yeah. Forgot that was today. How'd it go?"

"For goodness sake! It was a funeral. How'd you think it went?"

Lachlan shrugged. "Dunno. Just wondered what happened, like, did anyone fall out of a coffin or anything?" The two others laughed but Joel was furious and tried to keep his temper down.

"There were two coffins actually. One for Nadine and a small coffin for her child. Is that funny enough for you?"

Angus and Hamish stopped smiling and looked at Lachlan for direction. But Lachlan just smirked. "Cool down mate. It's not like they're your family or anything."

"Okay fine. If you die, I'll come to your funeral and laugh because, you know, it's not like you're family or anything."

Lachlan stopped smiling and there was a brief pause before Joel said, "Oh, forget it. It's been a rotten day." And with that he turned and continued on home where he planned to have an early shower and immerse himself in video games for the rest of the day and try and forget everything for a while.

Chapter 7

The weekend after the funeral was not pleasant.

Joel's mother, Olivia Kimball, spent both days glued to the front window as she watched a never-ending stream of people knocking on Ivan's door. But he never answered.

Olivia told Joel that she was concerned that something was wrong, but Joel thought that Ivan just wanted peace and quiet after such an emotional week. Who knew how long it would take him to get over the loss of his daughter and grandchild?

At night there were lights on at Ivan's house and they could hear his television because he seemed to have it on quite loud and his windows were open.

During the following week, Joel was busy at work while his mother still worried about Ivan. She tried phoning him a couple of times and went over and knocked at his door and called out to let him know who she was, but he still didn't answer at all.

At the garage, Ken tried phoning Ivan a couple of times every day, but he never answered.

Ivan was the topic of conversation with all their customers wanting to know how he was doing as none of them had seen him since the funeral and he hadn't been answering his door or his telephone. It soon became clear to the three mechanics that no one had seen Ivan at all. But they decided to tell people that Ivan was okay and still coming to terms with what had happened. They also told them that he and Owen were grieving privately together and just wanted to be left alone.

By the second week most people had stopped asking how Ivan was and Joel reported that the unending stream of people at Ivan's door had stopped, so clearly their message was working as it spread through the local grapevine. But by the end of the second week, they were worried because still no one had seen or spoken to Ivan.

Ken decided to get in touch with Owen to find out if Ivan really was as okay as they'd been telling everyone. He went into the office to call him.

A few minutes later he came back out and said that Owen hadn't heard from Ivan either. "He said he tried to phone Ivan a couple of times this week, but he didn't answer." He paused and then said, "I'm worried. No one's seen or heard from him for two weeks. It doesn't even seem like he's even gone out to buy groceries. Surely, it's not healthy for a grieving person to be so isolated for so long?"

"But what can anyone do if he won't answer his phone or open the door?" asked Joe.

Ken thought about it for a few seconds and said, "Ivan might not open the door to any of us but there is someone who he'll have no choice but to speak to or have his door kicked in."

"Who?" asked Joel.

"The police. We can report him as a missing person."

"But he's not missing. We see his lights go on in the house every night, so we know he's there."

"But is he okay?"

Joel shrugged.

"Exactly," said Ken and turned and headed to the office.

Joel thought that at 3 p.m. on a Friday afternoon, the police would be too busy gearing up to deal with after-work drunk drivers to worry about an adult who hadn't been seen for a fortnight. But he was wrong. Two policemen turned up within ten minutes of Ken putting the phone down.

Ken took them straight into the lunchroom to talk and Joel knew it was so that customers wouldn't see them and start asking about Ivan again.

After a while the police left and Ken came out. 'I told them that we know that Ivan's home, but no one has seen him or heard from him in two weeks and that he's not answering the phone or the door and so we're worried about him.

"I also told them about Ivan's wife dying two years ago, and of course they already knew about Nadine. So, they said we were right to be worried and that they'll go round to Ivan's house and do a welfare check."

"What if he still won't answer?" asked Joel.

"Well, I was right about them kicking in the door. They said that on a welfare check they HAVE to talk face-to-face with the person, so if he won't answer the door they'll break it down. But I'm sure he'll open it for them."

"Do you think he'll be annoyed with us for sending the police round?"

"No. Ivan's not stupid. He'll know we were worried. But right now we need to get back to work so we can finish on time."

It was less than an hour later that the police returned and said that Ivan was fine. He had allowed them to come into the house to stop passers-by staring. They said the house was a mess and Ivan was definitely hiding from everyone on purpose because he was still very depressed.

But nothing he was doing was illegal, so the police had left it at that.

Ken suggested that maybe he should call round and see Ivan from time to time, but the police said Ivan was adamant that he didn't want to see anyone and asked that they make it clear to everyone.

Joel later relayed this information to his mother, who was concerned about Ivan and thought that being alone was the wrong thing for him, whether he thought so or not.

The three mechanics continued to have no contact with Ivan, except for a couple of text messages that Ken sent him asking if everything was okay and to tell him that the business was fine and ticking over as usual.

Olivia Kimball, on the other hand, was sure that persistence would break Ivan's resistance and she spent the whole of the following week knocking on his door every day. She would knock several times calling out, "Ivan! It's Olivia. Are you there?" When she got no response, she'd say, "If there's anything you need just let me know." And then she'd offer to go and buy groceries for him or say he could come round anytime for a chat.

After a week she admitted defeat and stopped knocking. She concluded that it was clear that Ivan wanted nothing to do with other people at the moment, so she finally left him alone.

Two more weeks passed with no sign of Ivan anywhere. The customers were still asking about him and were told that Ivan was having some quiet time to grieve.

But it soon become apparent that Ivan was doing more than just grieving when the mechanics arrived at work one morning and found that a letter had been pushed under the door.

Ken had arrived within seconds of Joe and Joel who were waiting for him in the car park. They walked around to the front of the garage together and Ken unlocked the large roller door and pushed it up. There on the floor was the envelope. Ken picked it up and turned it over. "It's from a lawyer."

"Open it," said Joe eagerly.

Ken looked at it for a few seconds and said, "It's addressed to me. I'll read it in the office first." He sounded untrustful of what the letter might be. The first thought of all three of them was that it was a letter telling Ken he was fired. But why would Ivan fire Ken who'd worked for him for years? And why send it through a lawyer? And surely Ivan needed Ken more than ever now, so a letter, hand delivered from a lawyer was baffling.

Joe and Joel nervously began their day, turning on lights and unlocking doors, while Ken read the letter.

After only a couple of minutes Ken came out and showed the letter to the other two.

It was a request from the lawyer that all three of them remain after work the following day because the lawyer, Mr. Bradman, needs to have a meeting with them to discuss some legal matters. The letter seemed to raise more questions than it answered.

Joe looked worried and said, "Is someone suing us?" Ken shook his head "I wouldn't think so. The only place we're altogether is here so if it's a complaint from a customer I'd imagine they'd take it to Ivan, not us."

"Is Ivan suing us"

Ken shook his head in exasperation. "Ivan has no reason to take legal action against us, and for what?" He paused for a few seconds. "But it proves one thing for sure. Ivan wasn't just sat grieving all this time, and there's been at least one person he's been talking to, Mr. Bradman.

"What I wonder is whether this Mr. Bradman is his personal lawyer or his business lawyer. Either way, something's wrong."

"What do you mean?" asked Joel.

"People never get lawyers for a good reason. It's usually for when things go wrong or when they anticipate things going wrong, like making a will.

"But I have no idea why this lawyer wants to see all of us, not a clue, so we'll just have to wait and see. In the meantime, let's get back to work."

"I wish he was coming today so that we can find out what the hell is going on," said Joe.

"Me too" said Ken and Joel in unison. And then they all turned and silently got back to work.

The rest of the day was spent with more quiet times as all three contemplated what was going to happen and why Ivan would send a lawyer instead of talking to them himself. Joel told his mother about the letter while they were having dinner that night. She smiled and said, "That's wonderful."

"How is that wonderful? We don't even know what's going on."

"Exactly. You don't know why the lawyer wants to see you all, so no news is good news, as they say. And what is good is that Ivan hasn't been sitting alone being depressed as we all thought. Clearly, he's been doing something and talking to someone."

"Yeah, but what?"

The next day at work seemed to drag as they all waited till 6 o'clock so that they could close all the doors.

Once the place was locked up, they sat around the lunchroom table and waited. Within a few minutes there was a knock at the back door. Ken went to answer it and came back in with a man in a suit, who was about 35 years old and carrying a briefcase.

Ken sat down and indicated the spare chair to the lawyer who sat down and removed a folder from his briefcase and placed it neatly on the table in front of him along with an expensive looking silver pen, which he placed beside it.

"Hi, I'm Richard Bradman and I'm here because I've been instructed by your employer, Mr. Ivan Hubert. No doubt you're all eager to know what's going on, so I'll get straight to the point.

"Now I'm well aware of the recent tragic events in Mr. Hubert's life, and it's these events that prompted Mr. Hubert to make some changes in his personal and business life.

"I'm not at liberty to discuss these plans with you, particularly his personal plans, but I am here to tell you about how his business plans effect each of you and what I need you to do."

The lawyer paused there for a few seconds, for dramatic effect, Joel thought.

"Mr. Hubert hopes that you all understand his need to make changes in his life and one of the changes is that he has decided to sell the business. He said to tell you how much he regrets the need to do this but he's sure you will understand." Again he paused.

The three mechanics looked at each other.

Eventually Ken broke the silence. "So, what does that mean for us, I mean what should we do now? We've been running the business on our own for the last few weeks and even working overtime to get all the jobs done and keep the customers happy. Do we just carry on?"

The lawyer hesitated and took a deep breath before he answered. "No. You don't need to do anything. Mr. Hubert has instructed me to close the business immediately. I'm to collect all keys, computers and paperwork."

"But why?" asked Ken loudly making everyone jump. "I don't understand. If he's selling the business, then why close it?"

"Please," said the lawyer, putting up a hand to silence Ken. "I can't tell you why Mr. Hubert is doing things this way. I'm only here to deal with things on a legal basis."

"But we've got wages owed and holiday pay accrued."

"Yes," interrupted the lawyer, "and I was getting to that. In order to be paid the money you're owed, your time-sheets need to be up-to-date."

But ken was furious. Joel had never seen him like this before. "So, tell me this if you're here for legal reasons. Can he do this? Just like that?"

The lawyer remained patient. "Yes he can. As long as he pays all monies owed to employees and creditors and returns property, such as cars, to their owners, then he's free to close the business anytime he wants to. There's no law that says just because you own a business you're obligated to trade.

"Mr. Hubert is offering you all monies owed in unpaid salaries including holiday pay and one month's severance pay, as per your contracts. I'm sorry, but that's the law."

Joe flopped back in his chair. "I don't believe this. We've worked our backsides off keeping this place going for over a month now and this is how he repays us, by chucking us out?"

An ominous silence hung in the air with no one knowing what to say as all three mechanics struggled to digest this new information.

The ever-practical Ken spoke next and didn't sound as angry as he was before. "So, what happens now, I mean right now? You said you've been told to take our keys, so do you mean you want them right now?"

"Yes, the business is closed as of end of business today and I will be organising everything to do with the premises and assisting with the financial side of things so you will all be paid all monies owing, and so yes I do need you to handover all the keys to the property that are in your possession."

"So, I just give you my keys and we all just walk away and never come back? We're out of a job just like that?"

"I'm afraid so. I do have a copy of the written and signed instructions from Mr. Hubert himself if you'd like to see them."

"Yes I would," said Ken

The lawyer opened the file in front of him and efficiently picked up the top sheet of paper and placed it on the table in front of Ken.

He picked it up and quickly scanned the content. "Wow, that's short, sharp and abrupt."

"I'm afraid legal documents only pertain to facts, not emotions."

"Okay fine. Seeing as we don't work here anymore and we're wasting our own personal time right now, I'll go and get my keys." Ken put down the sheet of paper and pushed it back towards the lawyer, then stood up and left the room.

Joe and Joel sat silently and kept glancing at each other with neither knowing what to say. Ken was back in seconds with his keys in his hand. He removed one key from the ring and put it on the table. "That's the key to the big roller door at the front."

"Is this the only key you have?"

"The others are always kept here, plus Ivan has a set."

"And you two?" asked the lawyer looking at Joe and Joel.

Ken answered and he sounded annoyed. "They don't have any keys. They never had any keys. There was never any need because Ivan is usually here every day and when he isn't, which isn't often, I had a spare key. Now if there's nothing else, we need to go."

"No," said the lawyer. "There's nothing else you need to do here except collect any and all personal belongings before you go."

Ken turned abruptly and left the room, followed quickly by Joe and Joel.

At the lockers, Ken was pulling out all his belongings and stuffing them in his backpack. Joe and Joel likewise emptied their lockers too. None of them spoke until they were out the back door in the car park.

"What now?" asked Joe sounding helpless.

"Put your stuff in my car and we'll go to the pub."

Obediently, Joe and Joel followed Ken to his car.

It was a silent car ride to the pub, but once they were sat down with a drink they began to talk.

"This is unreal," said Joe.

"I know," said Ken. "How can Ivan do this to us? He just threw us out without any warning. And what was that about having to handover all the keys immediately? I can't believe that after all these years he doesn't trust me."

"It's weird isn't it?" said Joe.

"What's weird?" asked Joel.

"All this stuff with Ivan. It's like a rolling snowball that just keeps getting bigger and bigger.

"I mean it all started with him eating a dodgy sandwich and that made his daughter die and then he hides away for weeks and that made him close the business and throw us out on the street. You've gotta wonder what he's going to do next."

Ken and Joe were talking but Joel had stopped listening at the mention of the dodgy sandwich. He'd forgotten all about that. He'd forgotten that it was his fault because he'd tried to steal a sandwich from the shop and Algar warning him of the repercussions of every action.

And because he'd tried to steal the sandwich, the chain of events had ended with him losing his job.

Still not convinced, he still wondered whether his sandwich theft had really caused this seeming chain of events.

And in the back of his mind. His unconscious wondered whether this was the end of the events.

Or was there worse to come?

Chapter 8

'What does it take to get rid of people around here?' thought Ivan.

After the funeral he'd wanted to be left alone, but he was inundated with people phoning him, texting him and constantly knocking at his door. At first, he'd turned his phone to silent and kept quiet and pretended he wasn't home. But after the first couple of days he thought, 'Screw it. If they haven't got the message yet, then maybe I need to let them know that I'm here but I just don't care.' So, he turned up his TV to drown out the noise of people knocking at his door and turned his phone off altogether. It was ridiculous that everyone seemed to think that he needed their company. And no matter how much he ignored them they just didn't take the hint to get lost and leave him alone. He'd had to spend the first week surviving on what few groceries he had in the kitchen, but soon ran out, even though he hadn't been eating much.

During the next couple of weeks, people knocked on his door a lot less, so he took it as an opportunity to go out and shop.

But he still didn't want to see anyone, so he didn't go out till well after dark and drove to a supermarket a few kilometres away so that he wouldn't run into anyone who knew him.

He drove his car out of his garage with no headlights on so that the neighbours had less chance of seeing him. Once on the road he sped off quickly, turning his lights on as he went.

He bought enough food and drinks to last a few weeks and then went to a nearby off license to buy a few cases of beer and a bottle of whisky.

It actually felt really good to be out of the house where no-one knew him. He hadn't realised how cooped up he'd felt. So before he went home he went to a pub and had a beer, sitting quietly at a corner table so that no one would want to talk to him.

He sat and pondered his life. It had been so hard losing Nadine and the baby, and he'd cried a lot. That's why he hadn't wanted to see anyone. No-one could understand his pain, and no-one could help.

And now his tears had subsided and only flowed now and again instead of every minute of the day. So now it was time to think about what to do next, but he had no idea what he wanted to do. His tears may have stopped, but the sadness and emptiness remained.

There was one thing that he did know for sure and that was he was annoyed and angry, yes angry, that Ken had sent the police to his house because he hadn't answered his phone and was ignoring text messages. Damn him for doing that. But it had made him think about the garage and that made him admit to himself that he could never face going back to work again. He'd been in this situation before two years ago when his wife died. It hadn't been easy picking up his life again and trying to get back to some form of normality. When he went back to work it was hard to see everyone living their normal lives. Nothing had changed for them, yet he'd had to spend every day with a smile on his face, acting as though everything was okay, even though he was going home to an empty house and empty life every evening.

And now he'd lost his daughter and grandchild too. He knew he couldn't face dancing the same dance again, pretending things were okay when they really weren't.

The only way to avoid it was to not go back to work ever again. He'd have to close the business down. He felt a pang of guilt at letting the guys down that worked for him, but it was only a brief pang because nothing seemed to matter much anymore. The things that he thought were so important before, now seemed so insignificant.

He used to think that his business was one of the most important things in his life, now he felt differently. And if he closed the business the guys would be okay. They'd find other jobs. They were adults after all and were quite capable of looking after themselves. And if they couldn't? Well, that wasn't his responsibility.

Ivan finished his drink and headed home, parking his car quietly in the garage and closing the door immediately so that no-one would know he'd been out.

Once his groceries were put away, he settled down on the couch with a large glass of whisky. The TV was still on because he hadn't turned it off when he left. But he wasn't really watching it anyway, he was busy thinking about closing his business.

The next morning he phoned a lawyer. He had to turn his phone back on to do it and charge it up first. He saw that he had literally hundreds of missed calls, text messages and voice messages and he deleted them all without even looking to see who they were from. He didn't need anyone.

The lawyer agreed to come and see Ivan at home as he was familiar with Ivan's recent loss and his long-standing business, and thankfully, the lawyer seemed to be all about business and not about commiserating.

The lawyer arrived at lunchtime and talked through different options. Ivan was adamant that he just wanted to close the business first and worry about selling it later. The lawyer agreed and said he'd draft up a proposal for Ivan to sign later. Ivan was happy to let the lawyer deal with everything so that he didn't have to.

When the lawyer left, Ivan was relieved to be on his own again. He really didn't want to talk to anyone. He put his phone on silent and turned the TV back on again.

In the kitchen he opened his cupboards and scanned his groceries, pleased that he bought so many so that he wouldn't have to shop again any time soon, because leaving the house again didn't feel like an option.

Sitting in front of the TV with another glass of whisky, his thoughts turned immediately to his wife and daughter.

When his wife died, he had to be brave for Nadine, and although it seemed the hardest thing he'd ever have to do at the time, losing Nadine seemed harder because it would be so easy to wallow in his own grief with no one else to shield from pain this time.

So how, he wondered, was he supposed to cope? Two losses in two years was hard.

Tears began to trickle down his cheeks as he tried hard to think of what to do, of a way that would ease his sadness right now while time did it's healing.

He could always go to see a doctor and get some sleeping pills to help him sleep through his pain.

Or he could binge-watch TV and get so caught up in what he was watching that he would forget his sorrow for a while.

The other alternative was to drink enough alcohol to numb the pain, and if he drank enough, it would also help him to sleep more too.

Well at least he had choices, all of them were bad ones, but they were choices. A faint hint of a smile came to his lips as he wiped away the tears with his hand.

He went into the kitchen and looked once again at all the food he'd bought just to re-confirm to himself that he didn't need to go out and shop again for a while, because he didn't want to see anyone. Ever.

Even shopping out of town had put him on edge because there was still an outside chance that someone who knew him could have been there too, and he would have hated that. But at the same time it did feel good to be out of the house and doing something normal for a change. Although having said that, it had felt equally good to arrive back to the safety and privacy of his own home, so this was where he needed to be, at least until his sadness passed and he could feel somewhat human again. And he knew from experience that the heavy sadness does lift over time.

So the only remaining thing to think about was to make a choice about what to do in his immediate future. Going out was not an option. Neither was answering the door or the phone, except for his lawyer.

In his fuzzy mind he decided that alcohol was the answer. If he drank enough, it would ease his mind while he was awake by making it harder to think, and it would also help him to sleep a lot. It was a great plan and he may as well start straight away. No time like the present, as they say.

And with that he picked up the bottle of whisky and poured himself another drink.

That evening he braved going out shopping once more, only this time he needed to buy alcohol and lots of it. He figured the best place to go was to a liquor superstore, preferably one out of town.

So he drove several suburbs away which wasn't difficult to do at the coast because all he had to do was follow the road along the coastline for several kilometres and look for a large superstore, which were always well signposted.

Once inside he took a large trolley and filled it with whisky, rum, soft drinks, wine, beer and potato chips, as well as a few boxes of pre-mixed cans too.

Back at home he put as much as he could in his fridge and left the rest of the boxes and bottles stacked on the kitchen floor in the corner. That would do it. Now he had everything he needed close to hand to help him blot out the never-ending stream of thoughts and images of his daughter that paraded through his mind non-stop.

But this was it. He was going to put a stop to them. It was dark outside so all his curtains were closed and he was going to leave them that way, night and day because it didn't matter what time it was anymore. He was going to stop thinking sad thoughts by binging on TV shows and movies designed to lift his spirits, and the consumption of copious amounts of alcohol.

He poured himself a drink and sat on the couch in the living room. He used the remote control to sign into Netflix and looked for comedies. There were hundreds of them, TV shows and movies. So he chose one and settled back to let the booze and the comedy lull him into mindless oblivion.

Without realising it, he soon fell asleep. When he woke up, he could see that it was still dark outside but he didn't bother to find out what time it was. He didn't need to know. He just got up, poured himself another drink and chose another comedy to watch.

Yep. This was good. It was a great plan. Easy. Do-able. And most of the time he'd be asleep or too drunk to care about anything. Perfect. And he kept to his plan for the next two weeks.

* * *

"Ivan! Ivan!" The pounding on the door woke him from his alcohol-induced sleep. It was his son-in-law, Owen. "Ivan, I swear that if you don't open this door I'm going to kick the damn thing in!"

He sat up and looked around the room. He'd been asleep on the couch and the TV was still on and all the curtains were closed, but the light coming from behind them told him it was daylight.

He shouted to silence the noise. "Alright! I'm coming!" The pounding and yelling stopped.

Ivan got unsteadily to his feet and squinted at the clock on the wall. It was just after four o'clock. He must have slept all day.

He went to the door feeling wobbly, with his head pounding from a hangover and his mouth was dry.

As soon as he opened the door Owen stepped inside and turned to Ivan. "What the hell are you up to? People have been calling me to ask where you are, and I've been calling you but you won't answer your phone."

Ivan closed the front door and walked past Owen. "I need to use the bathroom." He carried on through the living room, went down the hall, into the bathroom and closed the door.

After emptying his bladder, which he discovered was long overdue, he looked at himself in the mirror while he washed his hands. He looked a mess. Dark circles under his eyes, hair so tousled it looked knotted, and his clothes so rumpled that anyone could see he'd been sleeping in them for days.

He dried his hands onto a now-grimy hand towel, flattened his hair as best he could with his hands, and took huge gulps of water from the tap. He then went back out to see Owen who was standing in the living room with the TV off.

Owen looked around the room in disgust and then looked at Ivan. "I really don't get it. Look at the state of this place. It's disgusting. I've never seen it like this. And you too. You look like you haven't showered or changed your clothes in weeks. And the smell here is disgusting, both you and the house."

"It's none of your business," shot back Ivan, unable to think of a better defense.

"Yes, it is my business," fumed Owen. "I'm the one putting up with all the questions from everyone asking what's happened to you. And by not answering your phone or your door it makes people worry. And I also heard that you shut your business and laid off the guys who worked for you. Why would you do that? Is it just so that you can stay home and mope?"

"I have my reasons."

"Yeah, selfish reasons. Look, if there's anyone who understands what you're going through right now it's me. I lost Nadine and the baby too. But I'm not stinking alone indoors and wallowing in self-pity about it. It happened weeks ago, and yes it still hurts and no I don't think I'll ever get over it, but what you're doing is crazy. You've lost your daughter, your grandchild and your business. If you're not careful, you'll lose a lot more."

Ivan was angry. "I don't care. How I grieve and for how long is my business and no one else's. Not even yours."

Owen sighed. "But the time for grieving is over. You'll never start to move on emotionally if you don't move on physically. Getting out and getting back to normal would be the best thing for you right now.

"Look, I felt the same at first. It was like nothing else mattered any more. But going back to work helped because it's the one constant in my life that didn't change. Nadine was never at work with me so for a short time every day I could grieve less. And it kept me busy at home too with all the paperwork.

"Going back to work seemed hard at first but it wasn't. Honestly Ivan I reckon that the longer you lock yourself away like this the harder it's going to be to get back to normal, especially since you closed your business too."

Ivan was livid. "Is that all you've come here for, to tell me how wrong I am and how righteous you are? Do you think I give a damn about how anyone else feels? I don't. Not even you.

"And I've lost more than you. Nadine was my daughter long before she was ever your wife. We grew really close after her mother died. It was a bond that you could never understand because you didn't go through it with her.

"So don't tell me how I should feel right now or what you think I should or shouldn't be doing. You've never lost a child, so you don't know what I'm going through. I lost my wife and now my daughter, that's twice the grief that you're going through that's why it's so easy for you to carry on so soon."

There was a few seconds of silent tension between the two men as they glared at each other. Owen's fists clenched and unclenched as though he was thinking twice about saying more. Then he suddenly turned and left, slamming the front door behind him.

Ivan felt his shoulders slump in relief. He didn't like confrontations, so he was glad it was over so quickly. But now what to do? It was only 4.30 in the afternoon.

He turned the TV back on and found another comedy show to watch. Then he went into the kitchen and took a ready-meal out of the freezer, put it in the microwave and mixed himself another drink, rum and coke this time. When his food was cooked, he took it and his drink into the living room and sat down to watch the whole final series of a comedy show he'd put on. And that was how his evening went on; drinking, eating, and laughing at the TV.

Next thing he knew he was waking up and he could see daylight coming from behind the curtains. He was slumped on the couch and the TV was still on. He turned it off, got up and stretched. He felt dreadful. So exhausted from doing absolutely nothing.

Looking at the clock he saw it was nearly half past eleven. Wow. He must have slept a long time, so long that he felt almost sober for the first time in weeks. He also noticed that he stank. He could smell his own BO and figured it must be time to shower and change.

The warm water felt good, and he had to admit that being clean felt so much better. He put his dirty clothes in the washing machine along with the few other things he found in the laundry hamper and then he went into the kitchen to make breakfast.

He ate a bowl of cereal and then some toast. As he sat at the kitchen table and ate his toast, washing it down with plenty of orange juice and black coffee, he thought about what Owen had said.

Maybe he was right and that if he started to go out and stopped hiding, it would make it easier to move on. Except that he didn't really want to move on. He wanted to go back. He wanted to have another do-over of that fatal night. He wanted to not buy the sandwich that made him too ill to drive Nadine home. He wanted her to be alive again. That was what he really wanted, but he knew it wasn't an option. He also knew that he didn't want to go out and speak to people. He wished he could just go outside and everyone would treat him like normal, as though nothing had happened, but he knew that wasn't an option either.

One thing that he could do though, was open some windows and let some fresh air into the place. Now that he was clean, he realised how smelly the house was. So, once he finished his toast and coffee he went around the house opening every curtain and every window. He even opened the front door but left the screen door closed and locked.

As he turned away from the screen door, he heard a car door close. He looked outside and saw that his lawyer had parked on the driveway and was walking towards the house.

"I wasn't expecting you" said Ivan as he opened the screen door.

"I have some great news, so I thought I'd come and tell you in person."

"Wow. Come on in."

Ivan took the lawyer into the kitchen where they sat at the table. The lawyer put the folder he was carrying on the table between them and placed one hand on top of it. "This is it. This is everything taken care of. Your business premises have been sold for full asking price to a guy who owns a whole string of garages and he's a cash buyer so once you sign the papers the money is yours... less my modest fee, of course."

Ivan smiled. "Well, I reckon the word modest is debatable, but that's wonderful news. I never thought the place would sell so fast. And I've owned it for so long. It'll seem weird to see someone else there."

The lawyer smiled and nodded. "I can imagine it will. And I've also been working hard for you on other things too, so not only did I draw up the purchase contract and have meetings with the buyer, but I engaged an accountant to finalise your business accounts and she's been working round the clock too. So now your business finances can be completed quickly once this sale goes through, AND the three guys who used to work for you have all been paid in full like you asked, so that's one major loose end taken care of."

It seemed strange to hear his employees referred to as "loose ends," but he guessed that's what they were. "So, what happens now?"

"You just need to read through the contract and sign it. It's a lot of legal-speak, but basically, it's saying that you're selling the garage and everything in it, and he's buying it "as is" with no comeback, guarantees or repercussions on you. It's what we call a whizzy-wig sale spelled WYSIWYG which stands for What You See Is What You Get."

Ivan had a quick look through the contract but didn't really read anything. He just flipped through the pages and signed each one at the bottom.

After the lawyer left, he sat at the table and tried to think. It seemed so weird to have signed his business away. The lawyer said that he'd have the money from the sale within the next couple of weeks. It all seemed so fast. But that was a good thing, right?

He sat and pondered what to do next. He didn't know what he wanted to do but he did know what he didn't want, and that was, he didn't want to live in Eden anymore because he didn't want to see anyone he knew or talk to them. They all knew too much of his personal business and he didn't want to discuss it with any of them.

So, in his mind there was only one thing he could do, and that was to sell his house and his car and start fresh somewhere else where no one knew him, and no one from Eden would ever know where he lived or be able to recognise his car.

This new revelation seemed perfect. Now that his family and his business were gone there was nothing to keep him here anymore, except his house. But once that was gone, he was free to go anywhere.

And he would begin his plan immediately.

Chapter 9

Ivan plugged in his phone and let it charge while he made himself some lunch. It wasn't that long since he'd had breakfast, but he was hungry and thirsty which was probably because it was several weeks since he'd had a drink without alcohol in it.

So, after consuming a huge plate full of greasy chips, onion rings and a few battered pieces of food, and washing it all down with two large glasses of soft drink, he put his dirty dishes in the dishwasher and looked at his phone.

It had charged up a bit and he saw that it was loaded with literally hundreds of text messages and missed calls. He deleted them all without even looking or caring who they were from.

He then used his phone to look up a local real-estate company and called them.

The young woman he talked to was very chirpy and said that someone could come and evaluate his house later that afternoon. Once again Ivan was surprised at how fast things were happening because he thought they would take a few days before they could come out.

Later that afternoon a middle-aged, plump yet efficient woman called Brenda arrived. He showed her around the house and she took copious notes about what she saw. Back in the kitchen, they sat at the table. "Well Ivan, the house is light and well set out and is a great place for a family. But there are a couple of issues that need sorting out, but if you could see to them promptly, then I'm prepared to offer your house at a high asking price."

"What are the issues?" asked Ivan cautiously, thinking that she was going to suggest things that would cost thousands to put right.

"Well, I don't know how to say this delicately so I'm just going to say it. This place is a mess. It's dirty and cluttered, and to be brutally honest it stinks in here. But I can also tell that once these issues are sorted, this house will look lovely. Also, your garden is overgrown and long overdue for a mow and tidy."

Ivan was relieved. "Oh, is that all? I thought you were going to suggest major changes or something."

"No. I just need everything to be presented as clean, neat, orderly and fresh."

"That's an easy fix. I can get someone in to fix all this straight away."

Brenda smiled. "That would be wonderful."

Next, they discussed the price, which wasn't much of a discussion because Brenda suggested a selling price that was far above what Ivan was expecting. So, the deal was set quickly.

The next morning the real-estate agent returned with a contract for Ivan to sign which he did, and then she said that she would only use an outside photo of the house and a floorplan for the marketing because the inside and the garden weren't ready for photos yet. Ivan couldn't argue with that.

When she'd gone, Ivan felt relieved that now the contract for selling his house was signed, it was one more thing that he could tick off his to-do list.

The next thing was to sell his car, so he opened his laptop computer and looked up how to do it. To his surprise it was relatively easy, so once he'd compared prices, he listed his car for sale on a local site. Tick. Another thing off his to-do list.

Next was to sort out his house and mow and tidy his garden, neither of which he wanted to do himself. But as luck would have it, his neighbour, Olivia Kimball, was walking by just then with a bag of groceries.

He rushed to the front door to try and catch her. "Olivia! Can I have a word?"

She looked both surprised and pleased to see him. "Of course Ivan. How are you?" She walked through his gate as she spoke.

"Oh, I'm fine, but I wondered if you could help me with something."

She put down her shopping bag and said, "Sure, if I can."

"Well as you no doubt know, I've been making a few changes in my life including closing and selling the business."

She frowned briefly. "Yes, unfortunately I do know, now that Joel is unemployed."

"Oh yeah. Tell him I'm sorry about that, but it just had to be done. Anyway, I'm also selling the house. In fact, I just signed the contract with the real-estate agent this morning."

"Oh, that's too bad. I'll miss you if you go. And this is all so sudden. Are you sure this is what you want to do? Where are you going?"

Ivan side-stepped the last question. "Yes, I'm absolutely positive that it's what I want to do. But what I wanted to talk to you about is to ask for your help in getting the house ready for selling."

"In what way?"

Ivan felt embarrassed. "Well, you see, the problem is that I've kind of let the place go over the last few weeks and now it's a bit of a mess and I don't know where to start with putting it right again.

"It's quite a big job and I'm willing to pay you. If you've got the time now you can come in and have a look and tell me what you think."

"Sure. Okay." Olivia left her bag of groceries on the porch and followed Ivan inside.

He showed her around every room and she almost had to hold her nose to block the smell. She knew that Ivan had been hiding in his closed-up house for several weeks and thought he might be living in a mess, but she had never considered that it would smell this bad. She could feel her gag-reflex trying to activate.

"So, what is it that you want me to do exactly? Do you want me to put everything away and clean through the whole place? That would be a full day's work. I'd also need to open all the windows to get rid of this smell. I'm sorry Ivan but it just really stinks in here."

"Yeah, I know. The real-estate woman told me that too. I just need this place cleaning and getting ready for viewers. Oh, and do you know someone who can also sort out my garden on short notice? It just needs mowing and weeding a bit, but I need it doing soon."

"Oh, I'm sure Joel will do it. He often looks after our garden for me. I can get him to sort out your garden while I do in here."

"How soon can you do it?"

"Well, I should be able to rearrange a few things and do it tomorrow if you want. But it really is a big job. I'll get Joel to help me once he's finished in the garden so we should be able to get finished in a few hours. But we'll need paying well."

"Oh absolutely. Money isn't a problem, and I can get out of your way while you do it too."

"That would be great. I can really get on with it quicker if I'm left alone to do it."

They agreed on a price and Olivia wasn't lying when she said she wanted paying well, but Ivan had no option because he needed the jobs doing quickly.

* * *

Olivia and Joel arrived promptly the next morning. Joel nodded at Ivan and said he would get the mower out and start straight away and he quickly disappeared into the garage.

Olivia was carrying a plastic bucket full of cleaning cloths, a bottle of spray cleaner and some polish and rubber gloves. "I'm going to start in the bathroom and then wipe down all the furniture and the kitchen and then vacuum and mop. I assume you have those two things?"

Ivan showed her where he kept them and grabbed his phone and car keys and left immediately as Olivia began to put on her rubber gloves.

He drove to a pub a couple of suburbs away and went in and ordered a cup of coffee and a plate of breakfast.

He took one of the newspapers from the corner of the bar and sat and read it as he ate his breakfast, which was really brunch because it was mid-morning.

When he finally finished reading the paper and closed it, he saw that the room was almost full of people and that he'd been sitting there for two hours. He also realised that this was the calmest he'd felt for weeks, which further confirmed his belief that getting away from Eden for good was the best thing to do.

He went to the bar to get a drink. As soon as he sat down his phone rang. It was Brenda calling to say that she had a couple that wanted to view the house tomorrow morning. Damn that was fast. He assured her that he already had someone taking care of the house and garden and it would be ready in time.

Then a few minutes later he received a text message from someone interested in his car and could they come and test drive it tomorrow afternoon.

Ivan stared at the message. It was so unbelievable how fast this was all happening. He thought it would take at least several weeks to sort everything out. Suddenly his feeling that selling up was the right thing to do felt wrong. He reasoned with himself that it was the right decision, and his unease was just because it was just happening too fast. Yeah, that was probably it. What he needed to do now was recover that laid-back, relaxed feeling he'd had earlier, so he ordered some lunch, picked up another paper, and sat and read while he ate.

After an hour he felt at peace again, but he had to think of what to do next. The house and garden would be ready for viewers tomorrow, but his car wasn't. He searched online on his phone for a car valet and found a place close to the pub where he was at the moment. Perfect. He called them but didn't hold out much hope of them being able to fit him in so quickly. But they said that they'd had a cancellation for tomorrow morning so he could bring the car in then. Not only that, but the appointment was for 10.30 which was 30 minutes after Brenda said she'd be there. It was starting to feel somewhat creepy at how easy and smoothly everything was happening. He booked the appointment and went to the bar to get another beer to drink while he sat and pondered the whole situation some more.

He'd never known anything that had seemed complicated yet turned out so easy to do. First his business was closed and sold without any effort, and now it looked as though his house and car were going to go the same way. But he shouldn't complain. People always told him that whatever you put out into the universe you get. And what he'd been putting out was strong feelings of wanting to sell everything he owned and move away. And now it felt like the universe was giving him a push. So it must be the right thing to do. Mustn't it?

He finished his beer and drove home. He'd been gone for hours and so Olivia should be finished by now.

When he got home he saw that his garden was neat and tidy and his house was gleaming inside. Olivia and Joel had certainly done a really good job and they were both still there, packing their cleaning stuff away.

"Olivia, it looks great. Thank you so much. You too Joel."

"Well, I won't lie," said Olivia. "It wasn't easy, but we've worked hard and Joel cleaned your windows inside and out too."

"Yes, I noticed. I didn't even know they were dirty till I saw them clean. Really, you two have done an excellent job and just in time too, I got a call today to say there is a couple coming to look at the house in the morning."

"You're kidding?" said Joel. "I thought you'd only just put it on the market yesterday."

"I did, but apparently the agent already had buyers in mind who've been looking for a house like this in this area so they're keen to view it."

"That's wonderful," said Olivia. "I think it will be weird to see someone else living here. Are you sure you want to leave?"

"Yep. Never been surer."

"Where will you go?"

"I don't know yet and I'm not even going to think about it till I leave. I'll probably rent somewhere for a while. All I want to do right now is sell the house and go."

Before Olivia could ask any more questions, he changed the subject. "And the first thing I need to do is pay you for all your hard work. Just tell me how much it is, and I'll go and get the money."

When she told him how much she wanted, he went into his bedroom and took out the cash that he kept at the back of his sock drawer. He counted out Olivia's money and put the rest back before returning to the kitchen to pay her.

He gave her the money and said, "I can't thank you enough for all you've both done today. You've done better than I could have. And Joel, I hope you find another job soon. If you need a reference, you only have to ask."

Joel nodded but didn't say anything.

Olivia picked up her bucket of cleaning materials. "Good luck tomorrow. I hope they like the place."

"Thanks."

And with that, Olivia and Joel turned and walked out the front door and were gone. Ivan was careful not to mess or dirty the house that night so that it would still look good for the viewers.

Brenda arrived promptly the next morning and was pleased with the transformation of the house and garden, and the lack of bad smell.

Ivan left almost immediately after her arrival and drove to the car valet servicing centre, dropped off his car and keys, and walked to the pub for a drink.

They said that the car would be ready in two to three hours, so he also had lunch while he waited. Being there again so soon gave him a Déjà vu feeling and just like the previous day, he felt relaxed and time seemed to pass by quickly.

Once home in the afternoon, he waited for his car viewer who also turned up promptly. It was a man who Ivan guessed was in his forties who said he'd recently returned home after working in the Middle East for a couple of years and needed a car as he'd sold his before he left.

Ivan went with him for a test drive and noted that the man was a very good driver. Once back at the house, the man looked the car over, including looking at the engine and said he'd organise a bank transfer of the money the same day and come back tomorrow to pick up the car. Ivan gave his bank account details and the man left.

Wow. That was fast. Now he was going to be car-less tomorrow. The guy hadn't even tried to negotiate a lower price.

He parked the car in the garage and as he was walking back into the house his phone rang. It was Brenda. She told him that the viewers had loved the house and she'd emailed them a 30-day contract which they'd signed and sent back so she had emailed it on to Ivan to print, sign and email back. "Isn't that great?" she asked enthusiastically. "They didn't even want to put a lower offer in because they've been looking for a while and so wanted to secure your place quickly."

"Yeah, it's great but it's so swift it's scary. But I'll go and check my email now."

"That would be wonderful. Any chance you can have a read through it and sign it today? That way I can collect their deposit straight away to really seal the deal."

"Sure. I'll do it now."

Ivan felt like he was in a dream as he went to his study to check his emails. Was this all really happening? Was he about to have no house, no car and no business? Well, it was what he wanted but right now the speed of it all was getting his heart pumping.

When his emails opened, there was Brenda's at the top of the list. He ignored the others and opened hers. Sure enough she'd attached a contact that was already signed by the buyers.

As instructed, he printed it, signed it, scanned it, and emailed it back. He didn't even bother to read it. He also emailed it to a local solicitor asking them to oversee the contact and sale of his property.

He then sat back in his chair and let out his breath that he hadn't even realised he'd been holding.

Well, that was that. The contact was signed, and he had to be out within thirty days.

A sudden noise made him jump. It was his phone alerting him that he'd received a text message. It was from the guy buying his car to say that he'd already transferred the money and he provided a reference number. He texted straight back thanking him and saying that he'd check his bank account later to make sure the money had been deposited.

He sat back in his chair. Wow. Just wow. He'd had no idea that he'd owned so many things that other people wanted.

It was time for a drink. It was only 4 o'clock in the afternoon but he didn't care. He needed a drink.

But as it often did these days, one drink turned into several, which was only interrupted by his need for dinner.

A few hours later it was dark, day had turn into dusk and then into evening and Ivan was still drinking.

He was sitting on his back patio with a glass of whisky in his hand and thinking about how strange it was going to be to see someone else drive away in his car tomorrow.

Driving his car out of the garage tomorrow ready for the buyer would be the last time he'd ever drive it.

But then a sudden thought struck him. The car wasn't gone yet so he could still drive it if he wanted to, except he'd had too much to drink now. Or had he?

He was pretty sure that he was still sober; relaxed but sober. Maybe.

Oh, to hell with it. It was his car and he could drive it if he wanted to. Surely it wouldn't hurt to go for a bit of a drive for the last time. What else did he have to do?

His mind was suddenly overwhelmed with grief over losing his daughter. It had been an emotionally tough few weeks and getting rid of everything that reminded him of his loss was a help and it had certainly kept him busy lately, but the truth was that his sadness still ran deep.

His shoulders moved up and down vigorously as he sobbed. When would the pain go away? Would he ever feel normal again? Was selling up just an attempt at running away from the hurt and sadness?

He didn't know. He wasn't sure of anything anymore. Except for one thing.

He needed to get out of here. He didn't want to sit and cry any longer. He needed to get away and he needed to do it now.

He wiped his eyes with the back of his hand, put his glass on the table, and went inside for his car keys.

It felt unusual to sit behind the wheel after he'd been drinking, because it was a thing he never allowed himself to do.

But tonight was different. He needed to drive away from here in his car for the last time. Tomorrow it would belong to someone else, but tonight it was still his.

He put the key in the ignition, started the car and reversed out of the garage. It still felt strange to be driving after drinking, but he was sure he'd be okay.

Once on the road, he drove along the coastline. There seemed to be a lot of traffic on the road, but he was certain he'd be fine.

But after about ten minutes he was uncomfortable with what he was doing and knew he wasn't driving well, so he turned around and headed home. In fact, as soon as he made the decision to stop driving, he felt the need to be back safely at home and realised what a stupid idea it was to think that he was still sober enough to drive. What he had to do now was just concentrate on driving till he got back to his house.

A few minutes later he turned off the main coast highway. Only a few more streets to go and he'd be home. He relaxed a bit, not realising how tense he'd been up to that moment. Nearly there. Nearly home.

Suddenly, he saw too late that someone was crossing the road in front of him. He tried to hit the brake to slow down, but he pressed down on the accelerator instead.

His car collided with the man with a sickening thud before he rolled over the top of the car and landed on the road behind.

Ivan took his foot off the accelerator and pulled up his hand brake, making his car screech to a halt in a 180-degree circle.

He leaned forward and peered out the windscreen at the lifeless body he'd left in the road.

Oh God. What had he done?

Chapter 10

Joel woke up slowly and without opening his eyes thought "Where am I?"

He could hear unfamiliar sounds, and even though his eyes were closed, he knew the room was light.

A hospital. It smelled and sounded like a hospital. But what was he doing there?

He opened his eyes and blinked a few times.

Turning his head, he could see that he was indeed in a hospital ward. There were three other beds in the room with a man in each.

One man was reading, one was watching TV, and the other was asleep.

Joel was confused. He tried to move but his whole body hurt. His left arm felt strange. He lifted it slightly, to see it. It was in a brace, the type of brace used for broken limbs. What the hell had happened?

He remembered being out with his three friends the night before, if it was actually only the night before, but that was all he remembered. How long had he been here? What time was it? Why was his arm broken? Why did his head hurt?

He was scared. Really scared. He didn't even feel fully awake. He thought that maybe this was all some kind of dream and soon he'd wake up back in his own bed.

But he knew it wasn't a dream. It was all horribly real, and frightening.

A familiar face suddenly entered the room carrying a cup of coffee and Joel felt all the tension flood from his body.

"Mum. What's going on?"

Olivia Kimball smiled at him, then started to cry. "Oh Joel. I'm so glad you're awake. I've been so worried about you." She sat on the chair on the right side of his bed, put down her cup, and held his hand. "Do you remember anything about that night?"

"I remember being in town with the Irish Trio, but nothing till I woke up here. This is scary. I don't know how I got here."

His mother wiped her eyes with her free hand. "You were hit by a drunk driver when you were walking home. The police came to tell me. You were unconscious in the road when I got there. I've never been so scared.

"The ambulance brought you here and they did x-rays and all manner of other things to find out where you were injured. It was a long night."

"Mum, you said did I remember what happened 'that' night. Wasn't it last night?"

His mother smiled sadly. "No. It was three nights ago. They said you might not wake up for a couple of days because you banged your head on the road, but I was still worried."

"Have you been here the whole time?"

"Almost."

Joel licked his lips and felt how dry they were. "I'm thirsty. Can I have some water?"

"Sure." His mother stood up and poured him a glass of water from the jug on the cabinet beside his bed. "Are you okay to sit up if I raise the bed?"

Joel had no idea. "I think so."

Olivia used the remote control to raise the top of his bed. Joel looked down at his arms and saw for the first time that there was a needle in his right arm attached to a machine holding what looked like a bag of some kind of fluid.

His mother saw him looking at it. "They've been keeping you well hydrated." She picked up the glass and offered it to him. He raised his right hand to take it and found it unnerving that such a simple movement felt so strange. "Thanks. Have I been in a Coma?"

"No, they just said you were unconscious. They also said you have multiple breaks in your left arm and leg and a few minor internal injuries as well as a few external bumps and bruises."

Joel felt frightened. "Did they say I'd be okay?"

"Oh yes," said Olivia with some hesitation. "But they also said you can't rush these things and that it could take some time before you're 100% again."

"How much time?"

"Maybe a few months."

"Months?"

"Yes, I'm sorry. They also said you may need surgery too, but at least you'll make a full recovery."

Joel didn't know what to say. It was hard for his brain to process all this new and unwelcome information. He raised the glass to his mouth and drank all the water in one go. It felt so soothing to his dry lips and parched throat. His mother looked worried. "Hey slow down. You don't want to make yourself sick."

Joel handed her the empty glass. "I needed that. This bag of fluid may be hydrating me, but it doesn't wet my mouth and throat. Did they catch the guy who did this to me?"

"Yes, and he was arrested. The police said that his insurance will cover all your medical bills."

"Was this his fault or mine."

"No, it was definitely his fault. He was drunk and should never have been driving."

She then quickly changed the subject.

"I brought a few of your things for you. I brought a few changes of clothes and your computer, your phone and some of your books. There's also some drinks and snacks too. They're all in this cupboard, but I doubt you'll be able to reach them at the moment."

"That's okay. I'll manage. Speaking of snacks, I'm starving. What time is it."

Olivia looked at her watch. "It's 11.30 in the morning. They should be bringing round lunch soon."

Joel was glad he'd get a meal soon. But he suddenly felt sleepy which was ironic after he'd only just woken up for the first time in three days.

Joel woke up to the rattle of the food trolley being brought into the room he shared with three other males.

His mother wasn't there. He must have fallen asleep while she'd been talking to him. One second, he was awake but felt tired, and suddenly he was waking up again.

There was a clock on the wall above the sink next to the entry to the room, it was 12.15, so he assumed it was lunch that was being served.

"Good afternoon Sunshine" said a plump nurse, putting a covered food tray on the standing tray at the foot of his bed.

"You must be starving, you haven't eaten for three days. In fact, I thought you were still asleep, but I saw you talking to your mother half an hour ago. Welcome back."

She came to the top of his bed and unhooked a remote control, that wasn't really 'remote' because it was still wired into the wall. "Let's sit you up so you can eat." She pressed a button on the controller and his bed began to lift him into a higher sitting position.

The nurse adjusted his pillows behind him then wheeled the standing tray to the side of his bed and swung it over his lap. She then poured him a glass of water from the jug beside his bed, put it on the food tray, said "There you go" then left, wheeling the food trolley out with her.

Joel used his one good hand to lift the silver cover from his plate. There was a good-sized helping of vegetable and bean lasagna with sides of roast potatoes and string beans. On a smaller plate, there was what looked like a small apple pie. He could tell it was apple because there was a small hole in the side crust and a piece of apple was protruding.

He didn't really care what they'd given him. He was hungry and it all looked and smelled great. He picked up the fork and started eating. He chewed slowly because every mouthful tasted good, and he wanted to enjoy it for as long as he could.

When he'd finished his last mouthful of apple pie, he laid back feeling like it was the best meal he'd ever had. Probably in normal circumstances the food would have been palatable at best because hospital food was never great. But because it was days since he'd eaten, his palate was fresh and unused, so the food tasted amazing. He closed his eyes.

"Joel Kimball?" the voice startled him. Opening his eyes, he saw a uniformed policeman standing at one side of his bed, and a policewoman at the other. It was the man who'd spoken.

He looked down and saw the standing tray was back at the bottom of his bed and the food tray was gone. How long had he been asleep?

He looked at the wall clock. It was just after two o'clock. Boy was he sleeping a lot. He was still sitting up. "Can you get me a glass of water please?" The policeman obediently poured him one from the bedside jug and Joel drank it in one go and handed the glass back. "Thank you. I need a nurse."

The policeman left and came back seconds later with a nurse. "It's private" he told the policeman. He and his partner left the room.

When they were out of sight, Joel said to the nurse "I need to go to the toilet."

He had no idea how long it had been since his last bathroom break, but he definitely needed one now. He also wanted a shower, so asked the nurse. She shook her head. "We can't let you shower, but I can wheel you to the bathroom and someone can sponge you down.

Ugh! That sounded awful, but his need was desperate because he felt filthy and his bladder was full.

It took quite a bit of maneuvering to get him into a wheelchair and down the corridor to the bathroom, along with his IV tube.

It was an embarrassing experience to have to be helped on and off the toilet and to have someone else wash him, but he did feel much cleaner, and they washed his hair and let him brush his teeth. They even dressed him in a clean hospital gown. The bandages and splints on his left arm and leg meant he was unable to wear anything else.

Once back in bed (and his sheets had been changed while he was gone) he felt so much better, even though moving had shown him how much pain he was in. A nurse also brought him a cup of tea and two pain-killing tablets which he gratefully swallowed.

He took a sip of his tea and placed it on the standing tray, which had been once again swung across the bed. The two police came back in, pulled up two chairs beside his bed, sat down, and took out their notebooks and pens.

The policewoman spoke first. "We hear that you only just woke up this morning."

Joel was unsure what they wanted. "Yeah, more like lunch time really."

"Do you remember the night of the accident?"

Joel took another sip of his tea, which tasted wonderful, just like his lunch. "I do remember that night, but only that I was walking home. The next thing I remember was waking up here and finding out I'd lost three days of my life."

The young policeman spoke next. "So you don't remember anything about the accident?"

Joel tried to think, to see if there was any suggestion at all in his memory that he remembered anything at all about a car accident, but all he felt was confused about waking up injured and in hospital and having no idea how he got there. "I honestly don't remember anything. Can you tell me what happened? All I know is that my mum said I'd been hit by a drunk driver and that he's been arrested."

"Well that about sums it up. You were crossing the road when the driver was so drunk and driving so fast that he couldn't stop in time, and we think he hit the accelerator instead of the brake because a witness said he speeded up. We have no reason to think he hit you on purpose so it must have been an accident that he accelerated."

"Why would he want to hit me?"

"We were trying to discover if there was any animosity between you and Mr. Hubert considering the recent circumstances of him closing his business and putting you out of work."

Joel was struggling to comprehend what he'd just heard. "It was Ivan who did this to me?"

The two police constables exchanged a glance. "I'm sorry," said the young policewoman. "We thought you knew who the driver was. Mr. Hubert was drunk at the time and thought he'd pressed the brake."

Joel didn't respond. His head was reeling with the news that it was Ivan.

The young WPC carried on. "Mr. Hubert was highly intoxicated at the scene and attacked the police who came to interview him. He was in such an agitated state that they had to restrain him which only made him more violent, so he was arrested and denied bail at his hearing the next day."

Joel finally found his voice. "So, he's still in jail?"

"Yes. Assaulting the police is a serious matter, as is driving with so much alcohol in your system. Plus, his house is about to be sold which makes him a flight risk as he'll have no permanent address and a whole lot of cash in his bank account from the sale of his business and his house."

Wow. Rich and stuck in jail, thought Joel. That has got to suck.

But at least what happened to Ivan was his own fault. It was just unfair that he had to drag Joel down with him. "First, he fires me, then he runs me over. Who would have thought that could happen?"

He then again thought about Karma but shook his head. Nah. There was no way that stealing a sandwich had anything to do with him losing his job and being hit by a drunk driver who turned out to be the same guy who fired him.

However much he wanted to deny it was Karma, he couldn't question the close timing of events.

* * *

The next morning a doctor came to see him.

"Hello. I'm Dr. Stephens. I'm a surgeon here and I worked on your injuries when you arrived."

Joel turned off the TV he'd been watching. "Oh hi."

"How are you feeling?"

"Not great. Every bit of me feels like it hurts. Will it heal soon?"

The doctor shook his head. "I'm afraid the answer is worse than no. Joel, you've been extremely fortunate with your injuries. They could've been a lot more serious.

"You see, you not only suffered the impact of the vehicle, but also the impact of your head and body hitting the road. Every bit of your body hurts because every bit of it was injured in some way. A lot of it's bruising, but you also broke bones and suffered internal injuries too. Not to mention the impact left you unconscious for three days, but at least your brain seems fine at the moment."

The doctor lowered his voice and spoke seriously. "Joel, I'm afraid it's going to be a long road to recovery for you, but I'm certain you will recover. Unfortunately, I'm going to do more scans and x-rays and you'll need one or two more surgeries.

"I patched you up the best I could when you first came in, but now it's time to look at how you're doing now compared to how you were and put everything right."

Joel didn't want to have more operations. "When will it all start?"

"Today. I'm going to set up some scans and x-rays this morning and hopefully I can fit you in for surgery this afternoon or tomorrow morning at the latest."

The doctor kept speaking but Joel had tuned out. He didn't want to go through all this. He just wanted to get better and go home, but clearly that wasn't going to happen any time soon.

* * *

Three operations and three weeks later Joel was still in the same hospital bed and still just as bored and fed up. The only good thing, if you could call it good, was that because of all the sedatives and painkillers he'd been taking, he'd spent a lot of time sleeping.

He'd had a few visitors, his family, his ex-work colleagues, but his memory was fuzzy. He knew his mother had been at the hospital a lot too.

He yawned and pressed the remote control repeatedly, looking for something on TV he might want to watch, but nothing looked interesting. Maybe he should ask a nurse to get his computer for him so he could at least play a game. He couldn't reach anything himself in the cupboard next to his bed, because he was still in a lot of pain and having his left arm and leg out of action didn't help either.

As he stared distractedly at the small TV screen hanging above his bed, he heard a voice beside him. "It's nice to see you awake for a change."

He turned to see a pretty young woman about his age standing beside his bed. She was holding the coloured string to a shiny round balloon that said, 'To Brighten Your Day,' and a box of chocolates.

"These are for you," she said cheerfully, putting the chocolates on the bed and tying the balloon string to a handle on the side of his cupboard.

The chocolate box had a little gift tag attached to it with the message "Joel, hope you're feeling better and back home soon. It was signed by one of his neighbours. "Thank you." Joel said.

"You're welcome." She said, smiling at him. "I deliver here all the time, but you're usually asleep. In fact, I think this is the first time I've seen you with your eyes open." She gave a little laugh and said, "Well, I'd better go and let you sleep." And with that she turned and left.

Joel watched her go.

"You shouldn't have let that one go, she's really cute," said the guy in the bed opposite Joel's.

"Couldn't stop her, mate."

The muscle bound man got out of bed and came over to Joel. "She's in and out of here every day, and every time she passes by, she looks at you. I reckoned for sure that when she came in this time you two would hit it off, but you let her get away."

Joel laughed. "Yeah right. I should've asked her to go out for a drink. I'm dressed for it." He tugged at his hospital gown as he said it.

"Yeah, but it would've been easy to get her into bed." He nodded at Joel's bed as he said it. Both men laughed. Joel said, "It's not often you meet a girl when you're already in bed."

They exchanged jokes and pleasantries a bit longer, but Joel's mind was still on the girl he'd just seen. There was something about her and he wanted to see her again.

His new hospital buddy said that she came to the ward every day. But the ward was made up of four open rooms with four beds in each, plus a few private rooms so he'd have to keep an eye out for her. And say what? He didn't know, but he'd think of something.

Being stuck in hospital had just moved from dull to intriguing.

Chapter 11

Amelia felt so excited she had to stop herself skipping out of the hospital ward.

She'd seen the young guy in the bed for several weeks now, but he was always asleep. She'd asked one of the nurses the other day who'd told her that Joel (yep, that was his name) had been in a car accident and had been unconscious for a few days and had since had several operations, so it was no wonder he was spending most of the time unconscious.

But now she'd finally seen him awake.

When she saw the balloon and chocolates were 'addressed' to his bed, she decided to deliver his last that day in case he was awake so that she could talk to him.

When she got to his bed, she was surprised to see him awake, even though she'd been hoping that he would be. Unfortunately, she got so nervous that she'd babbled a few words at him and left.

Damn. She should have played it cooler, but she'd gotten so nervous seeing him sitting up in bed. And she'd said something so dumb. She'd said it was nice to see him awake so she'd better go and let him sleep. How stupid was that?

And he hadn't said anything except thank you. Probably because he thought she was weird.

So, what now? She wanted to see him again. If she was lucky, someone else would order some gifts for him from the hospital gift shop where she worked. If not, she'd still pass by his room anyway and his bed was next to the doorway, so she'd see him.

Maybe she'd just smile and wave or stop by and ask how he's feeling.

Ugh! Why would she ask him that? People in hospital must get tired of that question.

She decided to just wait till she passed by his bed and see what happened. He was in the surgical ward and patients there received a lot of gifts ordered from the gift shop, so she knew she'd see him again. She just had to play it cool.

What was wrong with her? She'd never been this nervous around a patient before. She'd been doing the job for the last two years, since she was sixteen and had just left school. During that time, she'd delivered gifts to thousands of patients all over the hospital and all of them had simply been people she delivered to. She'd never thought of any of them as anything else, even the teenagers who'd tried to hit on her, which unfortunately happened quite a bit and it always made her feel uncomfortable and awkward.

But this guy Joel was different. He seemed extremely blasé about her being there and about his gifts. Maybe that's just the way he is. Or maybe he was still half-asleep after sleeping so long.

Either way it didn't matter. For some reason (and she had no idea why) she was intrigued by him.

To be honest, even when he was asleep all the time, she couldn't stop looking at him.

What it was about him that attracted her, she had no idea.

But she was attracted to him, and she had little butterflies in her stomach just thinking about him.

And she couldn't wait to see him again.

* * *

For Joel, the next few weeks seemed extremely busy, even though he was stuck in hospital with nothing to do.

He had a whole slew of visitors coming by including his mother, his neighbours, his ex-co-workers, the Irish Trio, his brother, his sister, and Amelia.

He'd gotten to know her after their first brief and uneventful first meeting, and she was the only good thing about what had happened to him.

Since the day she'd come to his bed to deliver the balloon and chocolates, he was hooked on her. He didn't know what it was about her. But there was just something.

The minute he'd laid eyes on her, he liked her, but he'd been so stunned by her sudden presence and so drawn to her immediately, that he'd been rendered almost mute and couldn't think of a thing to say to her.

Naturally, as soon as she walked away, he was annoyed with himself for his lack of verbal response and could think of a dozen things he could have said.

She was slim and pretty, with a really cute smile, but it was more than that, that attracted him to her. Usually, he didn't have much trouble talking to girls, although he was never as brazen as other guys, like The Irish Trio, although girls were never interested in them, despite how they saw themselves as God's gift to women.

It wasn't just females who weren't interested in The Irish Trio. Many males didn't like them either, so the three of them only ever had each other for company, except Joel. When he really thought about it, he only hung around with them because he'd known them since school, and if he was honest with himself (and while he'd been in hospital, he'd had plenty of time to think) he'd pretty much out-grown them. While he was moving on with his career and his goal of owning his own business, The Irish Trio still acted as though they were still at school and sat around doing nothing all day. They even talked like they were still at school and didn't seem to have matured at all.

This had all been brought home to him since they'd come to visit him in hospital a couple of times. They'd mucked around, poking into all the stuff in his bedside cupboard, swearing, clowning around on his bed and upsetting the other three men in his room. And the problem was that he was trapped with them in here and couldn't get rid of them until they were willing to go, and they were in no hurry to leave because as usual, they had nowhere to go and nothing to do.

It was sad that these three were supposed to be his friends, but just the thought of having them come visit again made him cringe. Maybe next time he'd tell them to be quiet. Or maybe he'd be out of here before they had a chance to come back again.

As he was sat up in bed thinking about his so-called friends, he heard the now-familiar rattle of the afternoon tea-trolley that they always brought around at three o'clock every afternoon.

The smiling tea-lady poured a cup for Joel and put a couple of biscuits on the saucer. She put it on his tray which was already over his bed. "There you go sweetie," she said with her usual smile. "Thanks Belinda. You spoil me as always."

She patted his good arm and said, "Only because you deserve it." Joel smiled at her. He liked Belinda. She was so sweet and motherly to everyone.

As she turned to go back to the tea trolley, Joel's mother arrived. Belinda had a ready smile for her too. "Oh hey, Olivia. I'll get you a cuppa."

"Thanks," said Olivia as she walked to Joel's bed. "Good timing."

Belinda set down another teacup with two biscuits on the saucer. "There you go love."

"Thanks. I'm ready for this."

"No worries," smiled Belinda, and then she was gone.

Olivia sat on the chair beside Joel's bed, picked up her teacup and saucer, and said, "How are you doing? Anything new happened?"

"No," said Joel. "The doctor came to see me as usual this morning and said I'm still healing as expected." He sighed. "I've been stuck in here for seven weeks now. It seemed bad enough when I had three operations in three weeks, but since then all I do is sit here everyday and hobble to the bathroom and back. At least when I was having the operations, I slept a lot of the time. But now without the strong pain meds, I'm awake and sick of being here."

"Well. You'd be no better off at home, because you still wouldn't be able to do anything, and they're worried about infection."

"Don't I know it. They still change my dressings every single day. And I still can't have a shower."

"Does it still hurt to walk? Is it getting any better?"

"No, it's no better at all. It hurts like hell. I still have to use the wheelchair and they have to lift me into it. My arm still hurts a lot if I move it, so I don't."

Olivia sipped her tea and said, "Let's hope you'll be out of here in the next week or two."

Joel sighed and leaned back against his pillows. "That sounds like such a long time."

Olivia put down her now empty teacup and nibbled on the biscuits. "Well, here's something to take your mind of things, Ivan's gone."

"What do you mean, gone?"

"Vamoosed. Disappeared. His house was sold while he was still in jail and when he got out, he left, and no one's seen or heard from him since.

"We now have new neighbours because a couple with two young children have moved into Ivan's place."

"So is Ivan still in Eden?"

Olivia shrugged. "Dunno. No one's seen him, so we all assume he's moved away. Even Owen doesn't know where he is. But he'll have to turn up eventually because it's his court trial soon. That will be interesting to see what happens to him."

Olivia stood up and picked up the teacups. "I'll see where the tea trolleys got to."

As she turned a familiar smiling face walked into the room, but the smile faltered as she saw Olivia.

Olivia's back stiffened. "Hello Amelia."

"Hi, Olivia," replied Amelia, waiting for her to move.

Olivia left with the cups and saucers and Amelia went to Joel. They kissed.

"I didn't realise your mother would be here. I'll come back later."

Joel held her hand. "It's fine. She doesn't hate you."

"Are you sure?" They smiled at each other. Olivia came back. Amelia walked around the other side of the bed and sat on the edge. Olivia resumed her seat.

Joel said, "Mum was just telling me that we have new neighbours. A family have moved into Ivan's old house."

"Oh great. Is that a good thing or a bad thing?"

What do you mean?" asked Olivia.

"I mean are they a good family or a bunch of noisy people."

"No," said Olivia "they're fine so far."

"Oh good."

There was an awkward silence.

"I only stopped by for a minute in between jobs, so I'd better get back to work. I'll come back in a couple of hours. Bye." She kissed Joel briefly, said, "Bye Olivia," and was gone.

"Mum, you could be nicer to her."

"Why? What's she up to?"

"She likes me."

"She works here. How do you know she doesn't like other boys too?"

Joel felt angry. "Just stop it, will you? I like her and I want to see her." He hesitated and added, 'and we're going to carry on seeing each other even when I leave here."

"Oh, you've discussed this have you?"

"Of course we have. She's been visiting me for the past month and the one big thing we have in common is that we'd like to spend time together away from this place."

"I suppose. "Olivia said resignedly. "It just strikes me as odd that she's latched onto a patient at the hospital where she works."

Joel smiled at his mother. "I see it as a cute 'how we met' story to tell our grandkids."

"Grandkids?" said Olivia, raising her voice in surprise.

Joel laughed. "It's just an expression, you know, a turn of phrase. The only future we've discussed so far is not meeting in a hospital ward every time we see each other."

"Thank goodness for that." She smiled at her son. She was worried that Amelia's interest in Joel would fade once he was out of hospital and she no longer had his undivided attention every time she saw him.

Only time would tell, but she didn't want to see him get hurt. His physical injuries were hard enough for him to cope with.

Olivia stayed with Joel for another half hour. She came to the hospital every day but didn't stay as long anymore as Joel got stronger.

Amelia arrived again at around five o'clock, smiling as always. She greeted Joel with a kiss. "Are we alone now?"

Joel laughed. "No, we're never alone. But if you mean has my mother gone, then yes, we're alone now." He did air quotes with his one good hand.

Amelia sat on the edge of his bed. "It upsets her to see me, doesn't it?"

Joel held her hand. "I think she's worried you'll steal me away from her."

Amelia looked at his broken arm and leg. "I don't think you're going anywhere anytime soon, stolen or not. Is she like that with all your girlfriends or is it just me?"

Joel was thoughtful for a moment. "I think it's more to do with how vulnerable she thinks I am right now. She was so worried about me when it happened and when I needed more ops, and I don't think she's finished worrying about me yet."

It was Amelia's turn to be thoughtful for a moment. "Maybe she thinks that I might hurt you more than any car ever could."

As soon as the words were out of her mouth she regretted saying them. Why had she said such a thing?

Joel went quiet and didn't respond. It was a huge awkward silence, and she didn't know how to break it.

Luckily it was broken for her by the arrival of the dinner trolley and a nurse shouting, "Meals on wheels."

"Sorry," she suddenly said. "I shouldn't have said that. I'm sorry."

"Move please." It was the nurse behind her with a dinner tray.

Amelia stood up so the nurse could put the dinner tray on Joel's standing tray and wheel it closer to him.

"I'd better go and let you eat."

"No," said Joel. "Stay with me for dinner. I'd share it with you, but portions aren't huge."

She felt so relieved that he wanted her to stay. "Alright. How romantic, staying for dinner."

Joel laughed. "I'm sure we'll do better once I'm out of here and I'm able to get around more. Just being able to walk would be nice."

Amelia smiled and clapped her hands together. "Won't it be great when we can go for a walk together? Other people have big dreams, but ours are simple. Just to be able to walk outside together and have dinner on our own."

Joel had been taking the covers off his food, but he stopped. "I'm sorry. This is no fun for you is it with me stuck in here like this." He suddenly looked miserable.

Amelia, once again, regretted her words, thinking, 'What the hell is wrong with me today? Why would I say something that makes him feel miserable about being stuck here?' She quickly tried to remedy what she'd said.

"No, I meant these dreams are good dreams. To anyone else, walking down the street together is nothing. It doesn't mean anything. But to us it will mean everything. It's going to be great. We'll always appreciate the little things while everyone else takes it for granted. We're the lucky ones."

"Lucky? Huh! I'm not feeling too lucky in here," and he smiled as he began eating his dinner.

Amelia was relieved that she'd put things right. What was wrong with her today? She really needed to think before she spoke, or make sure something really needed to be said before she said it, and if not, don't say it.

Poor Joel had enough to contend with right now with his painful injuries and being stuck in here. At least she could go home every night and sleep in her own bed.

She chatted to Joel while he ate his dinner, talking about everyday things and how she had to do a delivery to an old man who'd been in hospital for a couple of weeks, and when she got to his bed earlier this afternoon, she realised he was dead.

Joel stopped cutting a piece off his pie to ask, "How did you know he was dead?"

"At first, I thought he was asleep, so I was trying to leave the gifts quietly, but then I realised his face had sunken and gone sallow, so I went and told a nurse. She came and took one look at him and pulled the curtains around him."

"Oh gross." Joel carried on eating.

Amelia continued her story. "It's not the first time I've delivered to a dead person. It's happened twice before. My first thought is what a waste it was to send a gift. I guess I'm a bit practical like that.

"One dead woman had her husband sitting in the chair next to her reading the paper. As I walked away, I heard him saying to the nurse, "I thought she was quiet.""

Joel laughed and put down his cutlery. He'd finished his dinner. He took a long drink of water and said, "Speaking of closing the curtains, want to do mine?"

She smiled and got straight up. Closing the curtains around the bed was the only bit of privacy they ever got.

When the curtains were closed, she pushed the tray to one side and Joel pulled her onto the bed. She could only sit beside him because his leg was still sore. He kissed her passionately, one hand on her T-shirt caressing her breast.

She loved to feel him touching her, even if it was so limited.

She put one arm across his back and the other on the blanket over his 'good' thigh. He moaned in pleasure.

She slowly pulled away from him. "We don't want to get caught."

"We won't," he said, pulling her to him again.

The sudden noise of the curtain being pulled back made them both jump. A nurse came in with Joel's medication.

"Whoops, sorry to interrupt, but I've got Joel's fix for the evening."

'Thank goodness we backed off when we did,' thought Amelia, embarrassed that they'd been caught at all. Lack of privacy was a big problem.

Joel swallowed his pills. "Someone will be along in a few minutes to take you to the bathroom for your nightly ablutions," the nurse told him, "I'll straighten your bed while you're gone."

"Okay. Thanks," Joel replied.

As she left, the nurse pulled the curtains back and clipped them open.

Joel grinned at Amelia. "Well, that was a short and brief romantic interlude. Will you still be here when I get back from the bathroom?"

"Afraid not. I have to get home for dinner myself. Mum said she'll wait till I get home because she's ordering a takeaway. I want to have a shower before dinner so that we can play online after if you want to."

"Sure. Can you put my computer on charge before you go?"

"No problem." Amelia put his laptop on his tray and plugged the charger into the wall socket above his bed. "There you go. I'll meet you in the Promised Land later."

"See you there."

She kissed him and left.

As she drove home, she thought about their relationship. It was unconventional as hell, but it seemed to be working.

She ducked in to see him once or twice a day while she was working, whenever she was at or near his ward, and she visited him once or twice a week when she could avoid his other visitors, especially his mother, who really seemed to be threatened by her being there. She supposed it was because Joel had always lived with her, so maybe she didn't like another female coming between their mother and son situation.

But she still spent time with Joel when she wasn't at the hospital, when they met digitally in the online game, Journey To The Promised Land.

In the game they journeyed together, sharing items they collected along the way. Joel said he usually journeyed alone because he didn't trust anyone enough to journey with them and share his items.

Amelia was the same. Like Joel, she'd been playing the game a long time and never trusted anyone enough to play with them.

But they had a mutual trust of each other and that meant a lot to her.

They spent many evenings playing online together, helping each other through danger, working out the cryptic clues and storing everything they collected into a joint, digital, treasure chest.

So, although she and Joel weren't always physically together, they spent a lot of time in the online meeting of their minds and mutual trust.

She'd never met a guy like Joel before and their unique circumstances meant that they were spending a long time getting to know each other before their relationship could progress to being more physically intimate. And so far, she liked everything she was getting to know about him. She hoped he felt the same way about her too.

She was even getting to meet his family, even if it was only by accident. He seemed to have a close bond with his brother and sister, which was nice, and they seemed happy that he'd met Amelia.

She just wondered if things would be the same when Joel was better?

At the moment they'd settled into a Joel-is-in-hospital routine and when she was with him it was always in the exact same place, his hospital bed, and he had nowhere else to be.

What would happen when he was back in the real world?

When he had a job and friends to hang out with and family to visit? Would she still be part of his world, or would she become just a painful memory of his hospital ward?

She hoped that both of them being in the real world together would help their relationship, not harm it.

But would Joel being out of hospital make her see him in a whole new way?

And would he see her differently?

She suddenly realised that she was home, as she pulled onto the driveway. She'd been thinking so hard that she must have driven home on auto pilot. She hated it when she did that. What would have happened if she'd needed to brake suddenly?

That's how accidents happen. Damn. That made her think about Joel again.

She needed to stop the depressing thoughts. Besides she was hungry, and dinner would be delivered soon.

Then it would be time to Journey To The Promised Land with Joel.

Now that was a happy thought.

Chapter 12

Joel had gotten to know the medical staff and the auxiliary staff pretty well during his weeks of hospital stay. He also got to know many of the patients too. But most of them would leave and new ones arrive, except for a couple of guys who seemed to be more injured than him.

In fact, his wounds finally felt as though they were starting to heal. But only starting because he still couldn't walk unaided, but he had progressed to a metal walking frame and was managing a short walk around the room every day, plus he insisted on walking himself to the toilet. It was embarrassing to always have someone in the bathroom with him. They still insisted on walking with him, but they now waited outside. Sadly, he still needed help with washing himself down every day and washing his hair. Hopefully that wouldn't be for too much longer.

He'd been stuck in hospital for nearly three months now and it was starting to feel as if it was his new normal life. He was glad that his mother often said, "When you get home...." Her words reassured him that he wouldn't be stuck here forever.

He now also has a physiotherapist that he was taken to visit once a week. He didn't mind going because it was nice to get out of the hospital ward for a change, even if he was only being pushed in his wheelchair to the physio rooms. He also got to stand up and move around for a minute or two, and the therapist seemed to think he was doing well, which he guessed he was if he compared himself to a few weeks ago, when he could barely sit up without screaming in pain.

He was sick of wearing a hospital gown every day, but at least now they'd given him a cotton dressing gown (which unsurprisingly matched the hospital gown) and it was loose enough that he could get his heavily strapped arm into it.

The thing he was enjoying most about being here was seeing Amelia every day. He always looked forward to seeing her. Usually, in his pre-hospital life, he never spent time with anyone every day. He only saw his work colleagues on workdays and when he dated a girl, he only got together with her two or three times a week.

But with Amelia it was different. He was happy to see her every day of the week. Maybe it was because he had nothing else to do, or maybe it was because he really liked her. She was beautiful, great to be with, was always happy and smiling, and the real bonus was that she loved playing his favourite computer game. He'd been playing the game for months and so had she, so they had plenty to talk about, and they both learned things from each other about how to get through some tricky parts of the game.

And now that they were playing together and pooling their resources, it was even better playing it. It was like being on a date without actually being together. It was weird how his being in hospital hadn't affected them having fun together. Apart from all the personal touching which they were finding a bit of a problem in terms of lack of privacy, and his immobility and painful injuries. It frustrated the hell out of him. He wondered if it frustrated her as much too.

He tried not to think about it. There was nothing he could do about his predicament, so no point sulking about it.

He tried to focus on the TV. He'd been watching an old black and white sci-fi movie, that was funny because of the really bad special effects, but his mind had wandered. Lunch had already come and gone.

Suddenly Amelia was there.

"Hi," she said, smiling as she walked past his bed, unclipped the tie, and pulled the curtain closed.

Joel tried to smile, but he was unsure what was happening. He hoped it was something good.

Amelia sat on the edge of his bed and put her arms around his shoulders. He put his one good arm across her back.

"I miss you," she said.

Still unsure of what was going on he said, "I miss you too. What's wrong?"

"Nothing's wrong. I just wanted to be with you." She broke the embrace and held his hand. "I was just thinking about how we spend more time online together than we do in person, and when I am here, we have little to no privacy."

Joel looked worried, so she hurried on.

"I'm not saying it's a horrible situation, although it kinda is, just that even though we haven't had a normal relationship yet, I miss it. Does that make sense?"

Joel smiled at her. I was as though she could read his mind. "It's weird, but I was just thinking the same thing. I can't wait till we can be together away from here and on our own for a change. Two minds think alike, huh?"

"Oh Joel." She threw herself against him once again. They kissed passionately, as though they needed to make the most of what little private time they had together, which they did.

Amelia felt herself melting to his touch. She didn't care that it was two o'clock in the afternoon or that they were in a crowded and noisy hospital ward, she just wanted to be with him, feeling him touching and wanting her.

She slowly moved her hand from his back to his side and slid it all the way down to his hip, under the sheets.

Joel responded by moving his hand to her side, slowly moving it down to her hip, and then up under her T-shirt to her breast. He slipped his hand inside her bra. She stiffened and then let out a sigh as their kissing became more intense, more excited.

She massaged his hip with her hand, then moved it inside his underpants.

"Knock, knock. Joel are you there? Can I come in?"

Amelia broke away from Joel, her mind immediately thrown back into the present, into the sterile hospital room and Joel's mother arriving.

She felt annoyed. She had been so swept up in the sexually charged moment with Joel, that she'd completely forgotten about the rest of reality, which had come crashing in uninvited at the sound of his mother's voice.

She jumped off the bed and swiftly went to the other side, still hidden from Olivia's view by the curtain.

Joel did a heavy sigh, looked sympathetically at Amelia, and said, "It's okay Mum. You can come in."

As Olivia pulled back the curtain, Amelia slipped out the other side.

"Why is the curtain shut?" asked Olivia.

"Privacy," answered Joel abruptly.

Olivia looked at him quizzically. "What's wrong?"

"Nothing." He snapped. "I'm just sick of being stuck here. Everyone else can come and go, but I can't. I can't be alone either. At home I was in my room alone all the time, but here I've got nothing."

Olivia rubbed his arm. "I know sweetie. You've been here a long time, but hopefully it won't be for much longer. Just think how great it will feel when you finally get to leave here?"

But Joel didn't want to imagine it. He wanted to do it. He wanted to be able to have a normal relationship with Amelia, one where they could be alone, naked. Right now he felt more frustrated than ever and for more reasons than one.

He was afraid he'd lose Amelia if he didn't get out of here soon.

"It was Ivan's court case this morning. It didn't take long because he pleaded guilty, but then again what else could he do."

"Oh yeah, I forgot that was today. What happened?"

"Well, the judge wasn't happy with him at all, and called him reckless and irresponsible, and was disgusted that you'd been injured so badly that you were still in hospital.

"He sentenced Ivan to six months prison, but with time served and parole, he might only be in there for three months, which is disappointing because it's not much is it?"

Joel was silent.

To him three months was a long time. He'd already been stuck in hospital for well over two months and it would be a couple of weeks yet at least before he'd get to go home.

So, he and Ivan were both being locked up for three months for what he did.

It really wasn't fair.

Amelia felt bad that she'd upset Joel by rushing in to see him and complaining that they couldn't have a normal relationship. But it turned out that he didn't like it either and it ended well with an intimate, yet extremely brief make-out session on the bed. Who knows how far they would have gone if his mother hadn't arrived?

She visited him for an hour or more once or twice a week, usually in the evening, but that was usually the busiest time of all because everyone else had visitors too.

But now it was more than two weeks since their brief encounter and Joel was finally going home.

He'd texted her that morning to say his doctor had given him the last-minute check-over and signed him off as an inpatient. His injuries were far from healed, but he was mobile now and so sick of being in hospital that they were letting him go home. His mother was coming to pick him up in the afternoon, and Joel had just texted again to say she was on her way, so Amelia was off to say goodbye to him.

When she got to his room, she saw he was dressed in shorts and a clip-up shirt. It occurred to her that she'd never seen him dressed before, only in his hospital garb.

"Well don't you look amazing," she said as she approached him.

He looked up. He was in the middle of taking his belongings out of his bedside cabinet and putting it all on the bed.

"Hey, you made it," he said, giving her a quick kiss. "I wasn't sure if you'd be busy working or not."

"Oh, I've got a few more deliveries to do this afternoon and some to get ready for tomorrow morning, but I didn't want to miss your big moment."

Joel sat on the edge of the bed and patted the space beside him. Amelia obediently sat. "What's up?"

Joel looked serious. "We've talked a lot lately about how great it's going to be to see each other away from this place, but we never talked about immediate things. After I leave here today, when am I going to see you again?"

Joel looked unhappy. "The problem is that even though I won't be here, I'll just be at home instead. I still can't go anywhere, and I'll be relying on my mum to do everything for me. So, we'll really only be exchanging this prison for another prison."

"Can't you go anywhere at all, even if I drive you?"

"No. The doctor said it's better if I stay at home and stay off my feet as much as possible, except for my daily walks for a few minutes. If I fall or overdo it and I'm not at home, I'll be in trouble. And I can't go in a car because I can't bend my leg enough plus there's the seatbelt issue. So, we can still only meet in one place. But we haven't said where."

He was right. They'd forgotten to discuss their immediate future when they would see each other again once he'd left the hospital.

"You never said you'd be stuck at home. I thought we could at least go for a drive or drive to the pub or a café. So, we still can't go anywhere?"

"I'm sorry, but I didn't know either until this morning. I thought we could drive places, but it seems not. And when I thought about it, the doctor's right. I'd never be able to get in and out of a car or stretch my leg out inside it. And moving around is still difficult. But at least we'll have more privacy at my place."

"How? You live with your mother."

"Yeah, but she's had a TV installed in my bedroom and bought me an adjustable bed, so at least we can be alone in there."

Amelia wasn't convinced. She'd imagined picking Joel up and driving off in the car with him. She could take him to her place to meet her family and go get a takeaway and have a nice picnic near the beach, listening to the ocean. They lived at the coast, and he hadn't seen the ocean for weeks, nor would he for several more.

"So do you want to come to my place tomorrow night?"

Joel's voice broke her out of her reverie. She felt wounded that he didn't want to see her tonight. "Tomorrow night?"

He held her hand. "Yeah, I thought it'd take me tonight and tomorrow to get used to being back at home, plus you're working tomorrow anyway."

Amelia was disappointed. "So, you don't want to Journey To The Promised Land with me tonight either?"

"No, not tonight. It's going to be too weird, and I don't think I'd be able to concentrate. But I promise that tomorrow night, I'm all yours."

Amelia felt like she was going to cry, and she didn't know why. "I feel like it's over. We've always been together here and now you're going and I'm going to be left here without you. It's going to be weird."

"Hey, let's not get down about this, me going home is a good thing. It's what we've been talking about and looking forward to for weeks. "And it's only one night, and I promise that tomorrow night you'll have my undivided attention. I'm not thrilled about being stuck indoors for several more weeks either, but at least I'll have my own room."

"I don't think your mum's going to be too happy about me turning up all the time."

"Are you looking for reasons not to see me?"

"No. of course not. It's just that your mum works from home, so she'll always be there."

"Even if she didn't, you work all week anyway. Besides, the fact that she's home all day is one of the reasons they're letting me leave. They're organising a nurse and physio to come and see me all the time so that will be during work hours too."

He took both her hands in his. "Don't worry. I'll see you tomorrow night and we'll take it from there."

He looked at his stuff on the bed. "Mum will be here soon. Want to help me pack?"

"Sure." She got up and started putting all his clothes in one backpack, and his computer and accessories and books in another. There was also a lot of paperwork."

"What's this?"

Joel grinned. "It' seems you're talking to a wealthy man."

"What do you mean?"

"Before I came here, I was getting dole money since I lost my job. But the accident meant that I could trade up to temporary disability benefit which was more money. And because I've been stuck in here, I've spent almost zero of it, so it's been piling up in my bank account."

"Seriously? Wow. I never thought about you getting money while you were here. That's brilliant."

"It was Mum who did it. She had to get in touch with them because I couldn't sign on every two weeks and they told her I needed to change my welfare claim because I was no longer fit for work. Not a bad deal is it? They're paying me to lay around in bed all day."

"You'll be even richer by the time you are fit to work again."

"And I'll get other things like free prescriptions and other stuff. And while I'm laughing about it, I'd much rather not be in this position, but I can't think about it, or I'll start falling down the self-pity hole again. Onwards and homewards."

He looked past Amelia and smiled. "Hi Mum."

Amelia turned to see Joel's mother coming towards them. She forced a smile. "Hi Olivia."

"Oh hey, Amelia," she said chirpily. "Today's the big day that my boy finally comes home." To Joel she said, "I've just spoken to the nurses at the desk and asked them if they could organise an ambulance and it turns out there's one available now. So they'll be here soon."

She took out a keyring with three keys on it and handed it to Joel. "Just in case the ambulance gets there before me, which I doubt, here are your house keys."

Joel took them and tucked them into the front pocket of his computer backpack.

Olivia walked around Amelia and gave Joel a gentle yet all embracing hug. "It's so good that you're coming home. I've been rattling around there on my own for far too long. And no more hospital visits. I'll not be sorry to never have to come here anymore.

"I did a ton of cooking last night and made all your favourite food. I even made those cookies you like, and I haven't made them for ages."

She'd released her hug as she spoke. Joel smiled at her and seemed genuinely pleased.

"THAT is amazing. I thought I was looking forward to your cooking instead of this hospital food, but now I can't wait. This day just keeps getting better."

Just then two paramedics arrived. "You must be Joel. We've come to whisk you away from this evil place."

Joel smiled broadly at them. "I bet not many people are happy to see you guys, but I'm ecstatic."

"Come on. Your chariot awaits. Let's not waste any more time."

Amelia stood motionless and miserable as she watched everything going on around her, but she wasn't a part of it.

The two paramedics pushed Joel's wheelchair to him. He sat in it. His mother picked up his two bags and the four of them left.

Joel looked at Amelia as he was wheeled by and said, "See you tomorrow. I'll call you."

And they all disappeared around the doorway and out of sight.

Right there, right then, Amelia wanted to sit on the floor and sob her heart out. Joel was gone and it felt like she'd never see him again.

She stood there for what must have been a full minute, trying to contain her emotions and walk out of there with dignity.

Just when she thought she'd pulled herself together, two nurses came in carrying clean bed sheets and cleaning material. They chatted happily, oblivious to Amelia and began to strip the sheets off Joel's bed.

It was more than she could take. It was like they were getting rid of any trace of him being there, which, in a way, they were.

Amelia walked out as fast as she could before anyone could see her tears start to flow.

Once out of the ward, she left by the emergency stairwell, and sat on a step and howled.

Chapter 13

The following evening, Amelia drove to Joel's house and parked on the driveway. He'd warned her that his mother always parked in the right side of the garage so she could park on the left side of the driveway.

She took a few deep breaths before she knocked on the door. Joel had called her that afternoon and said he'd talked to his mother at length about Amelia being a regular visitor, and though she wasn't enamoured with the idea at first, he said she did accept it.

Olivia opened the door and gave a non-committal smile. "Hi Amelia. Joel's in his room. I'll take you through."

She said it without emotion. No friendly chit-chat. Nothing about how Joel was doing. Just announcing her duty of having to show Amelia where Joel's room was. "Thanks," she said stepping through the door.

Joel was in a bedroom down the hall, sat up on his adjustable bed. He had a tray on wheels, just like he did in hospital and his computer was open on it. He looked up and smiled as she came in. "You're here at last. How weird is this? I don't think we haven't seen each other for this long before."

Amelia went to him and bent to kiss him. He pulled her onto the bed and kissed her passionately. She pulled away and turned around, unsure if Olivia was still there. "Don't worry. She's gone," he assured her.

He pushed the tray away to make more room. Amelia asked. "Did you steal that from the hospital?"

"No, Mum got it for me. Apparently, there's a lot of stuff you can buy for old people and crippled people, and this is one of them."

Amelia put her arms around Joel and hugged him as tight as she dare without hurting him.

"You feel so good," said Joel. "I miss you." Amelia broke the embrace. "Those are the best words I've ever heard."

Joel looked confused. "Why? Did you think I wouldn't miss you?"

"I did kinda."

"Why?

"Well, you've come home to your normal life, something I've never been a part of."

He took her hand. "You've been a part of my life for a long time now. For a while, you were the only good thing about it. Having you was what kept me from dropping into a deep depression, because no matter how bad or painful it all was, I had you to look forward to every day."

Amelia started to cry, not audibly like she had the previous day when he left the hospital, but the tears still flowed.

"Hey, why are you sad? This is a great time for us. Look around. There's no one else here but us. I don't have to share a room with three more men and a doorway that's always open."

Amelia laughed and tried to halt her tears. She wiped her face with her hands. "I was just so worried that you wouldn't want me anymore because it's all so different now and we won't be seeing each other every day like we used to. It's like we had a hospital life, but now it's different in the real world."

Joel said slowly, "Close the door." Amelia obeyed and then came back and sat on the bed. Joel picked up a remote control and pressed it. The other side of the bed raised up into a sitting position. "Come sit with me properly. We're not in hospital now."

Amelia went to the other side of the bed, kicked off her shoes and sat beside him. It felt weird to be completely up on the bed with him, they'd never done that before.

They turned to each other and kissed deeply. Amelia had to turn more towards Joel than he could towards her, but she didn't mind.

He put his arm around her, pulling her closer, then let his hand slip to the side of her waist under her T-shirt. She let out a small moan of pleasure. His hand caressed her side then moved up to her breast cupping it inside her bra.

She moved one of her hands to his thigh and stroked it. Joel's body stiffened. They were both aroused. They'd been in this state before but had never been able to progress any further.

Joel's hand moved over her breast, squeezing gently and fondling it lovingly.

Amelia moved her hand up his thigh. He opened his legs as she moved her hand between them. His loose pants allowed her to easily feel his erection. His kiss became harder.

She pulled away, removing her hand from between his legs. "We can't do this."

He removed his hand from inside her bra. "Why the hell not?"

"Your mother could walk in any minute."

As though on cue, there was a soft knock at the door. "I'm making coffee. You two want a cup?"

Amelia giggled at the timing.

"Sure," Joel said.

"How do you take yours Amelia?"

"Just black, no sugar. Thank you"

Joel looked at Amelia in amazement. "We just can't catch a break, can we?"

"You could've said no to the coffee."

"She only would have come back and asked if I want tea or a cold drink. It's what she does."

Amelia laughed. "Ah, the voice of experience."

"If I say no to one thing, she thinks I want another. It never occurs to her that maybe I don't want anything. Except you," he said, putting his arm around her and trying to pull her close.

Amelia got off the bed, walked to the other side and sat on the edge. "I don't think it will look too good if she sees me up on the bed with you."

"I don't care. She's going to have to get used to it."

"Let's be cautious and not rock the boat too soon."

Joel thought for a few seconds and said, "Yeah, you're right. This is weird for all of us. But it's so frustrating. I want to be alone with you. REALLY alone, and not with my mother sitting down the hall."

"Me too," said Amelia miserably. "Me too."

* * *

Amelia agreed to come back and see Joel in a couple of days. She didn't want to turn up at his place so often that his mother would get sick of her. At the same time, it would be hard not to see him.

The days in between, they talked on the phone, texted, and played Journey To The Promised Land.

She arrived at his place at 7pm exactly which was the time they'd arranged.

This time Olivia seemed happy to see her. "Hi. Come in. He's down the hall as usual."

"Thanks," she said, walking past a smiling Olivia. This time she didn't escort her.

Joel also looked unusually happy to see her. She kissed him. He patted the other side of the bed and said, "Come and join me."

She looked back at the open door. Joel said, "Don't worry about that. Mum and I have come to an understanding and she knows that you'll be joining me on the bed because it makes it easier and because there's nowhere else to sit in here apart from my desk chair over there."

Amelia was skeptical. "Really?"

"And it gets even better. I talked to her about shopping because she says she doesn't want to go out and leave me on my own. She was going to shop online and have groceries delivered, but I convinced her to do the shopping while you're here."

"You're kidding."

"I kid you not."

Again, as though on cue, Olivia appeared in the doorway and said, "Right, I'm off out to get a few things. Call me if you need me."

"We'll be fine, "said Joel.

"See ya." And she was gone.

They sat silently listening to the sound of the car door close, the garage door opening and closing and Olivia's car driving away.

"Alone at last,' said Amelia.

"Close the door," said Joel.

Amelia did so, then kicked off her shoes and hopped on the bed beside Joel.

This was it. They finally had the privacy they'd been craving.

They embraced and kissed long and hard, both of them free to enjoy each other's body.

Amelia relaxed into his arms, wishing it could be both his arms and knowing that intimacy was going to be somewhat awkward, but she was going to enjoy it all the same.

Just like the other night, Joel moved his hand to her bare breast, and she moved her hand between his legs, feeling instantly how excited he was.

She broke the embrace and pulled off her T-shirt, unhooked her bra and slid it off.

Joel gazed longingly at her breasts.

She kneeled on the bed facing him and said, "How do you want to do this?"

He grinned and said, "I'm going to need a bit of help, that's all."

* * *

Amelia glided out of Joel's house that night after their long-awaited physical encounter. It wasn't as awkward as she thought it might be, and on a sexual scale, it was even better than she'd imagined. Also, so unexpected. She thought that it might have been weeks before they got any time alone. Luckily Joel had convinced his mother to go out, which, she suspected, suited Olivia too, to be out of the way when Amelia was there. No doubt she knew what Joel was up to.

Her visits to see Joel carried on in much the same way over the next few weeks with Olivia sometimes going out, and she and Joel spending more intimate time together. She loved laying naked in his arms after sex, and she wouldn't have felt comfortable doing it if they weren't alone.

Olivia had also warmed to Amelia and treated her like an invited guest rather than an interloper between her and Joel.

It had been Joel's twentieth birthday a couple of weeks ago and Olivia had organised a family and friends get together and invited Amelia too.

Joel's family had been so nice to her and were happy to finally get to know her. It was heartwarming to be treated like one of the family, as though she belonged with them.

Joel was out of his bed for his birthday and sat in an armchair on the back patio, and everyone gathered around him.

Amelia pulled up a chair next to him and he held her hand a lot. She could tell that he wanted to keep hold of her hand, but with only one good hand, he needed it for drinking and eating too.

The birthday gathering ran through late afternoon and into the evening. Joel wasn't supposed to drink because of the painkillers he was on, but he had a couple of beers anyway and so did Amelia. It was the first time they'd ever had a drink together.

Amelia was hoping to have some private time alone with Joel afterwards, but she could see that he was exhausted, so she left at the same time as everyone else.

It had been her nineteenth birthday a couple of weeks before that, but she hadn't told Joel until after, because she knew he wouldn't be able to celebrate it with her or go out and buy her a gift, and it wouldn't have been the same if his mother would have gone out and bought it and given it to him to give to her.

Instead, she'd celebrated it with her family at a local restaurant when they all went out for dinner. None of them had ever met Joel. Their relationship had been strange in a lot of ways right from the start. And not only had she never dated anyone for this long, but she'd never not brought them home to meet her mother.

Her mother always asked how Joel was doing. Even though she'd never met him, she was well aware of what happened to him because he and Ivan had been the topic of local conversation for a long time.

At least now she could tell her mother that seven months on from having his accident he was finally getting better. He was doing so well that his mother had bought him a walking stick, and he was able to use it. And it was far better than needing the walker that he'd been using before.

On this bright and sunny Saturday afternoon, she was off to see Joel.

When Olivia opened the door she said, "Hi, he's out back traversing the garden. Come on through."

Amelia went straight to the patio door in the dining room and saw Joel making his way incredibly slowly around the garden. She went out to join him.

He was pleased to see her, but he looked tired. "How's the stick working. Can you do a full circle yet?"

He stopped and said. "Not yet. This is my first go."

"How long have you been out here?"

"About fifteen minutes or so. Turns out it's a lot harder than it looked. I'll be glad when I get back to the patio."

"I'll walk with you, and you can tell me all about your day."

Joel started walking again, leaning heavily on the cane. "Well, it began well when I walked myself to the bathroom this morning. It took a lot out of me though.

"The good news is that I'm on minimal pain killers now, so I only need to take them when necessary. Bad news is that at some point every day, it's necessary.

"The extra good news is that my casts are going to be taken off next week. I'll still have some supports for my arm and leg, but it will only be light, and I'll have more of what they call freedom of mobility.

"The bad news is that even without my casts, I won't be able to tap dance, but that's okay, because I never could."

They both laughed at his attempted humour.

"Well progress is progress and you've come a long way to the guy I first met in hospital who couldn't get out of bed on his own."

They were now back at the patio. Joel went straight to the armchair and sat down. "I could do with a cold drink. Can you get me a glass of orange juice?"

"Already done," said his mother coming out with two glasses of chilled orange juice and ice."

Joel looked at Amelia who had sat down at the table next to him. "I have no idea how she does that, but she keeps doing it. Thanks." The last word was to his mother as he took a glass of juice from her hand.

"You're welcome." She placed the other glass on the table in front of Amelia.

"Thank you."

"Enjoy," she said, walking back inside.

Joel took a few big mouthfuls of juice and said, "You're right. I have come a long way since the accident, but I still wish I was back to normal. The physiotherapist said I'm almost there and that I'll realise it when I get my casts off.

"I have to go back to the hospital to have them removed and for more x-rays. I hate going back to the hospital, it makes me shudder every time. Probably because it reminds me of the bad old days when I was imprisoned there."

"Well, it wasn't all bad. We met there."

"True."

"It's funny, but even after all this time I still think of it as your bed. Whenever I go in that ward, no matter who's in that bed, they always look as though they don't belong there because it's your bed."

Joel laughed. "That's funny. I left that bed knowing I'd never see it again, but I forgot that you still go there all the time. Why had I never thought of that?"

"Probably because I think about it enough for both of us. I even had to deliver gifts to the person in that bed a few days after you left. It felt wrong."

Joel laughed again. "It's weird how I know you work at the hospital and I saw you delivering to my ward all the time, but it never occurred to me that you still go there all the time."

"That's because you have more important things on your mind like getting better so that one day we can actually go out somewhere together."

Joel finished his juice in one big gulp and put his glass on the small table next to his chair. "I was thinking that exact same thing yesterday, and I thought that after I'm unshackled from these chains that still bind me, if I'm able to sit in a car, we could take a drive. Not far. Maybe to the beach, so I can hear the ocean again. Maybe we could get a takeaway and eat it in the park by the beach.

"Honestly, I've missed normal life so much you wouldn't believe it. In fact, if it wasn't for you, I don't know what I would have done. You saved my sanity."

Amelia knew that he meant that as a compliment, but it didn't sound like one. What she heard him say is that he had needed her a lot when he only had bad things going on in his life.

And it all came back to, would he want her around once he was well again and good things started happening in his life for a change.

She felt so conflicted. On the one hand she couldn't wait for him to be better so that they could finally, after all these months, start having a normal relationship.

On the other hand, his recovery was a bad thing if it meant he would neither need nor want her anymore.

Right now, she knew he was sincere and that he really did want to be with her.

But things could and usually did, change.

* * *

Joel had his shackles removed and as predicted he could now travel by car, but only short distances, but it suited them fine.

Amelia came to pick Joel up one night. Olivia was agitated and worried that something would go horribly wrong. She followed them out to the car in what seemed like a last ditch effort to get Joel to change his mind.

"Just remember that just because you're feeling fine doesn't mean you are. You've been taking it easy and that's why you feel good. If you overdo it you'll be right back where you started."

"Mum, I'll be fine. We're not going far and we're only going to sit a few steps from the car, so I'll be hardly walking at all."

"But it's uneven ground and it's dark. You could trip on something"

"I know. I'll be careful."

"Amelia, look out for potholes when you're driving and speed bumps."

"Mum, for goodness sake, she knows how to drive. Do you think either of us wants me to be injured again? I just need to get out of here for a change."

Amelia was waiting for Joel to get into the car, but it seemed to be taking him a long time. She was standing at the open driver's door watching Joel over the car roof. His mother's panic was driving her crazy.

She got into the car saying, "Don't worry, I intend to take good care of him."

After another frustrating thirty seconds or so Joel finally made it into the passenger seat.

"Don't forget your seatbelt," said his mother as he shut the door.

Amelia started the car and said, "Please don't open your window."

"Don't worry, I wasn't going to," Joel said as he fastened his seatbelt. He gave his mother two thumbs up as Amelia reversed off the driveway and headed up the road. It felt so strange having Joel in the car with her. In fact, it would be strange being with Joel anywhere except his place and hospital. "Where to?"

"I have no idea," he told her. "Surprise me."

She took him to the drive through of her favourite Mexican fast food place.

"What do you want to eat?" She asked as they pulled up to the speaker.

"Surprise me," he said again, so she ordered two burrito bowls, a portion of chips and two drinks, which they took with them to the park.

Amelia pulled into a parking spot right at the edge of the narrow park that wound its way for miles along sand dunes at the edge of the beach.

They got out of the car and walked a few steps to a covered picnic table. It took Joel several minutes to do this whereas it used to take seconds.

He sat on the bench seat and laid his cane next to him. Amelia sat opposite and got the food and drinks out of the bag.

She put the carton of hot chips in the middle of the table to share.

Joel stared out across the sand. "Listen to that. Doesn't the ocean sound great?"

Amelia had always loved the sound. She'd lived at the coast all her life, and couldn't imagine not hearing it regularly.

"It's beautiful."

"It's the sweetest thing I've heard in a long time. Even just the simple drive here and going through the drive-through, it all feels so amazing, and it used to feel so ordinary. It's like I just dreamed about them before, but now they're real. Just being here tonight is so...so... I can't explain it. It's unbelievable."

Amelia took the lid off her bowl. Joel did too. They ate in silence with Joel constantly looking around him, amazed at every sight and every sound and she could see him keep sniffing the salty sea air.

Suddenly he said. "I want to do this again. Let's come back here again next week."

"Sure. Are you okay? You seem different."

He paused briefly, then said, "I'm just loving every minute being here with you. My first trip out in months and it couldn't be better. Me, you, the ocean, the food. What more could I want?"

She smiled at his child-like enthusiasm, glad to be part of an experience he'd never forget.

The following week they repeated their outing and sat at the same table by the ocean eating a burrito bowl, only this time they talked.

"I wish we could go for a walk on the beach," said Joel.

"So do I."

"Do you miss it too?"

"Only with you. I've walked on the beach plenty of times. I've just never done it with you."

"Have you done it recently?"

"Yeah, a couple of weeks ago."

"Any other times since my accident?"

"Of course, I've walked, sunbathed and swam too."

"You never told me."

"I didn't want to upset you. It seemed unfair to talk about things that I could do that you couldn't."

"Anything else you've been doing without me?"

Amelia wasn't sure how to answer. "I feel like you're accusing me of having fun without you."

"Have you?"

"Joel, I work full-time, and I've spent a lot of time indoors with you or playing online with you. So, if I want to go to the beach, I will."

"I'm not saying you can't, it's just odd that you never mentioned it."

"This is starting to feel like an inquisition."

Joel was quiet, and then he said, "It's weird, but it feels like you've been cheating on me with the beach."

Amelia didn't really understand. "How did you think I was keeping up with my tan? Did it not occur to you that I was spending time outside? What's wrong with you?"

"I don't know. It just felt like being at the beach was new for both of us. I forgot that you have a life apart from being with me. "Just ignore everything I said. I don't know what's wrong with me."

"You're right. I do have a life outside of us. I also have a family that you've never met. How about coming to meet them soon? How about this weekend?"

"Sorry, that's too fast for me. I need to get used to my freedom first before I meet new people."

"It's been eight months."

"I know. You've been ultra-patient with me, but I just need more time."

It turned out to be another month before he met Amelia's family, but by that time he was walking much more and much better.

Amelia's mother instantly liked Joel. Amelia thought it was because he was still injured so it made her feel motherly towards him.

"So, Joel, do you have any plans to sue Ivan?" Amelia's mother asked him.

Joel was taken off-guard. No one had ever asked him that. "No. Why would I?"

"You've been injured and unable to work all this time. You must have lost a lot of money, not to mention all your pain and suffering."

"Ivan's had pain and suffering too. He lost his wife, his daughter and his unborn grandchild. He was a decent guy. I don't want to add to his problems."

"I'm sorry. I'm sure your right, but if he'd done this to my child, I'd never forgive him." Then without missing a beat she changed the subject. "I made a cake. Amelia told me that you like chocolate cake, so I made one. You drink coffee too, don't you? I'll go and get us all some coffee and cake." She whisked off into the kitchen before Joel had time to answer.

The house was open plan so they could see Amelia's mother busy in the kitchen getting everything ready.

Amelia said, "I'm sorry she said anything about you suing Ivan. It's just that she thinks it's unfair that you've suffered so much from something that's not your fault."

"I think it's unfair too, but it brings me down if I start thinking about it. I need to stay away from the woe-is-me type of thoughts. Being forced to sit around all the time gives me too much time to think and my thoughts can get dark pretty quick if I let them."

They were sitting on the couch. Amelia leaned over and kissed him.

"Now, now," said Amelia's mother, "save that for when you're alone." She was putting cups and plates on the dining table. "Come and take a seat."

Amelia and Joel got up and sat at the table. Amelia's mother brought the coffee pot and the cake and cut everyone a slice and filled their coffee cups too.

Joel picked up his fork, cut a small piece off his cake and ate it. "This is delicious."

Amelia's mother beamed. "Thank you. That's so nice."

Joel had learned a long time ago that whenever someone made him some food, to eat some straight away and say it was wonderful. It was a way to get into anyone's good books, and he definitely wanted Amelia's mother to like him. Her cake really was delicious too, so he didn't need to lie.

When they all finished their cake and were sipping coffee, Joel said, "I got some good news from my doctor and physio this week. They both agree that I'm ready to walk further than around my own garden."

"That's wonderful," said Amelia's mother.

Amelia looked happy too. "Does that mean we can go out for a walk?"

Joel smiled back at her. "Yes. In fact, they said to only go out in the daytime so that I can see potential trip hazards, and to always have someone with me. So, I will need your help."

Amelia was ecstatic. "I can't wait. We can finally be seen out in public together. And yes, before you say anything, I know I've been driving us to the park every week for nocturnal picnics, but it's not the same. I can come to your place, and we can actually walk out the front door together."

Joel was happy that she was so pleased. "I'll still need my trusty stick, of course."

He patted the walking cane leaning up against his chair. "But the even better news is that they said there's no reason why I won't make a complete recovery and eventually start walking unaided again. I just have to regain the muscles in my leg and arm and then I'll be okay. It will take a few more weeks, but then I'll be fine."

Amelia was so glad that they'd be able to do something normal like walk down the street together. She saw other couples doing it all the time and felt envious.

She'd supported Joel all the way through his recovery, and she always would. But sometimes she just wished they could be a normal couple doing normal things.

And finally, it was happening. This was a good thing. So why did she have little pangs of worry, worry that as he gained more independence, he wouldn't need her anymore?

Chapter 14

The first time they left Joel's house together, they were both smiling broadly at this new experience. It was also new for Amelia as she'd only ever driven away from his house.

"This is so much better than walking round your back yard," she said, beaming.

"Well, it's only a short walk around the block for now, but who knows? We'll eventually travel the world."

Amelia laughed at his lame attempted humour. "You've been stuck at home for a long time. I had no idea injuries could take this long to heal."

"Me neither, but my leg and arm were pretty messed up. I'm just glad I can't remember it actually happening."

"Does it still hurt?"

"Strangely no. It does hurt a bit, but it seems more stiff than anything. It's as though my leg and arm have forgotten how to work.

"It's like I have to think really hard to get them to move too, which they said is part of the nerve damage which takes a long time to heal. Also, my tendons have shrunk somewhat through lack of use, so I have to teach them how to be stretchy again, but not too quickly or I'll damage them. Am I impressing you with my medical knowledge?"

"A bit, yeah. I didn't know anything about tendons before."

"Me neither. Half the stuff the doctor and physio say to me I don't understand, so I just nod."

"I guess you don't need to know everything, just the basics like not over-stretching your tendons."

"Yep, I just want to get better and get my life back. I want to have a better life with you so we can go out for burgers and swim in the ocean during the day and walk on the beach at night."

Amelia was so happy that he wanted a future with her. She knew he meant what he said now. She just hoped he'd feel the same later.

"You know," he said, "I'm still envious that you have a beach life without me."

Amelia felt her heart sinking. "Not this again."

"I know you have every right to do what you want when we're not together. I'm just jealous because I can't be a part of it."

She stopped and looked at him angrily. "Are you always going to be this controlling?"

"I'm not trying to control you. I'm just saying I'm jealous that I can't come with you."

"Who said you ever can come with me?"

Joel looked concerned and a little confused. "But I just said I can't wait till we can go to the beach together. What's wrong with that?

"What's wrong is that you assume that once we can go together, I can never go without you."

"Whoa. I never said that."

"Yes, you did. You said you'll be a part of my trips to the beach alone. But you won't. I'll still go to the beach on my own whenever I want. Yes, we'll go there together, but times when I'm not with you, I'll do what I want."

"Stop. Just stop." Joel sighed. "I think I said it wrong. What I meant was whenever I think of you going out and enjoying yourself without me, I'm envious because I can never come with you. I don't plan on spending every minute of the day with you anymore than you plan spending every minute with me.

"I just know that I'm missing out on us having fun together, and it hurts. And... sometimes I wonder if you'll get bored with waiting for me. There's plenty of able-bodied guys out there yet you're stuck here with a cripple."

Amelia didn't know what to say. She felt mixed emotions of being humbled because she'd misunderstood what he'd said, suspicious because she wondered if she had misunderstood, sad at his confession of feeling vulnerable and annoyed at his self-pity.

So, she said, "Do you trust me?"

"Of course I do."

"Then stop being jealous and feeling sorry for yourself. It's pretty insulting that I've stood by you through what must be one of the most difficult and painful times of your life, and you're doubting me."

Joel took a few seconds to respond. "Amelia. I'm sorry. I shouldn't have said any of that."

"Yeah, but you're thinking it."

"Wouldn't you if the roles were reversed and you were hobbling around with a walking stick, while I'm out living my life?"

Amelia let out a heavy sigh. "I guess. I think that we both know that things will be different when you're up and around again. We just don't know how different."

"Let's just see how it goes and never speak of it again."

Amelia smiled. "Agreed. Can we get back to our walk? I was really looking forward to this, but the fun seems to have gone out of it."

Joel turned to face forward and began his slow walk. "Me too. It feels so good to be out and about, skipping along the street."

"Skipping?"

"Well, I know it seems like I'm going real slow, but in my mind I'm as fast as a race car."

"Were you ever that fast?"

"Always. In my head at least."

"Come on then speedy. Let's keep going."

They continued their upbeat conversation for the rest of the short, yet long walk. It was a warm and sunny day, which added to the happy feeling of walking out together for the first time.

They continued to take a lot of walks over the next few weeks. They often walked to the park near the beach and sat and watched the ocean, enjoying the sound of the waves crashing on the beach.

They also walked to the fast food restaurants and enjoyed meals together and went to the pub for a drink a few times, but only for one drink at a time because Joel had to be careful.

At times it almost seemed that things were normal especially when Joel no longer needed to use his walking stick.

The regular walks helped him to make good progress.

The day he decided to no longer use his cane, he was cautiously optimistic. He was already walking around the house and garden without it, but they were short walks, so not very challenging.

On longer walks with Amelia, and walks to the supermarket with his mother, he found that he wasn't leaning on his cane at all. It seemed like more of a habit to have it with him whenever he went anywhere.

So, he made a decision not to take it with him anymore. It was a day that his mother was going out to get a few groceries.

"I'm coming with you, but I'm going to walk normally. No stick."

"Are you sure?" his mother asked him. "I mean really, really sure?"

"Yep. I need to do this."

"Okay. Let's go then."

They got ready and left the house together. Joel felt glad to be walking without his stick yet at the same time it felt strange to be without it. It had gone everywhere with him for months. Physically he felt fine without it. Emotionally he still felt attached, as though there was something missing.

His mother broke his reverie. "It's a beautiful day today. And I don't want to spoil it, especially with you walking unaided for the first time in ages, but today is exactly a year since Nadine was killed."

The news hit him with a jolt. "Are you sure?"

"Yes. Exactly one year ago is when it all started to go horribly wrong. First Nadine and her baby died, then Ivan went into a depression, sold his business, put you out of work, then got drunk and hit you with his car. It was a terrible time that I'll never forget."

"Me too," he said, but he was thinking about the other thing that happened that night one year ago, when he was caught trying to steal a sandwich from the shop. Such a stupid thing to do. Why had he ever let his idiot friends talk him into it?

The store manager had said that what he'd done would produce bad karma, and certainly a lot of bad things had happened since then, but if all things are equal, then his injuries were far worse than the theft of a cheap sandwich. It wasn't even a theft because he got caught, but he did destroy the sandwich so although it never left the shop, it couldn't be sold.

He'd almost forgotten about the sandwich incident, which wasn't surprising considering all that had happened since then.

One good thing that came out of it all was that he'd met Amelia. And that was a direct result of everything that had happened. So maybe it was a case of 'all's well that ends well' except that it didn't end well for Nadine and her family.

But none of it had anything to do with that damn, stupid sandwich, apart from it all began on the same night, but he couldn't see how else it was all connected.

He continued his walk of freedom with his mother and helped her do the shopping and carry the groceries home. They chatted amicably the whole time, but he couldn't stop thinking about trying to steal the sandwich and all the events that had unfolded afterwards. It had all been a strange and overwhelming time in his life.

He thought about it the rest of the day, despite trying to distract himself playing computer games and watching TV.

Why couldn't he get it out of his mind? He realised that he'd never set foot in that shop since that fateful day. Maybe it was time he went back there for another visit, and what better day to do it, than the one year anniversary of when it happened.

His mind was made up. He'd go there, not only today, but at the same time he did a year ago. He used to finish work at 6 o'clock, so that's what time he'd go.

He told his mother that he didn't want dinner because he was going out and would get something later.

"Joel, you haven't been out on your own yet, why don't you wait till tomorrow and go out when it's light."

"No, I want to go out now. I'll be fine. I can walk just as well as I used to."

"Where are you going?"

"Just out. I haven't been out on my own for months. I need to do this."

"Okay, fine, but don't stay out long. You know I'll worry."

"Well don't. I'm not a baby."

Are you seeing Amelia?"

"No. I told you, I just want the freedom of being alone for a change."

"Fine. I'll leave you alone." And she did.

At 6 o'clock exactly, Joel said goodbye to his mother and left. It felt strange leaving the house on his own, but it also felt good. As he walked down the street, he was acutely conscious that he was alone. It was strange how something so simple and natural now felt alien and unnatural. At the same time, it felt great to have the freedom to be on his own and go wherever he wanted, although right now he only wanted to go to the small supermarket where it all began.

He continued his short journey one conscious step at a time. He felt so free.

Before he made it to the shop, he ran into his three friends, the Irish Trio, which gave him a feeling of Déjà vu because it was exactly what happened a year ago and what got him into trouble.

"Hey, look at you," Lachlan greeted him. "When did you learn to walk again?"

The other two sniggered.

"It's taken months, but I'm good as new, in fact better than ever."

"Good," said Hamish. "We're going for burgers and you're paying."

"Why should I pay?"

"Because you haven't been out with us for ages, so it must be your turn to pay."

"Actually, the last time I went anywhere with you guys was exactly one year ago, and it didn't end well."

"Why? What happened?" This from Angus.

"You talked me into going with you to steal sandwiches, and I got caught."

Lachlan sneered. "You still pouting about that? It was your own stupid fault for not getting out of there quick enough. We had a plan, but you blew it."

"You left me behind. Anyway, I'm on my way there now, and this time I don't want you three losers with me."

Lachlan threw his hands up. "Why the hell are you going there?"

"I just want to. It's exactly one year since that night and it was the same night that Nadine Hubert was killed and then other things happened after that, including me ending up in hospital. So now I'm going to go back there, and bad stuff ISN'T going to happen.

"Says Who?" asked Hamish.

"Last time I got caught and the manager told me that karma responds to everything and me doing one bad thing could have negative consequences that come back and hurt me."

The other three burst out laughing. Lachlan said, "So what terrible things happened because you tried to take one pathetic sandwich?"

"How about Nadine dies, I got run over and Ivan went to jail."

"Bad sandwich," said Hamish wagging his finger at Joel in mock disapproval.

Joel was unperturbed. "I don't care what you guys think. Weird things started happening that night. My life was so normal before that. I even lost my job. Nothing in my life has been the same since then. And tonight is the first time I've gone out on my own and without a walking stick. And if that's not enough, it's like my being better has happened exactly one year to the day it all started to go wrong."

"Yeah, you're right," said Hamish. "It's exactly one year since the day you lost your frickin mind, you idiot."

"Oh, come on," protested Joel. "You've got to admit that the timing of it all is way too spooky to dismiss it."

"So let me get this straight," laughed Lachlan. "You're going back to the shop tonight to try and undo some sort of voodoo that the hippy manager put on you?" They all laughed mockingly.

"What the hell are you talking about? I said that the timing of everything was a spooky coincidence. I never once said anything about voodoo."

"You know what?" said Hamish, putting a hand on Joel's shoulder. "You used to be fun. Now you're just boring. We asked if you wanted to come for a burger, but you're too busy messing with karma voodoo stuff. What happened to you? Maybe it was your head that got damaged too."

Joel felt angry. "Tell me this. For the past year I've been in hospital, struggling through several painful operations and going through physiotherapy and doctor's appointments and taking strong painkillers and working hard to get my life back so that I can get another job and continue my plan to run my own business one day. I've achieved a lot.

"What have you three done apart from being dole bludgers back then and still being dole bludgers now? I've also had a girlfriend for the past year. How about you guys?"

"Yeah, so what?" spat Lachlan. "You're unemployed too now, so you're no better than us. At least we've been having a good time."

"Great. Go pay for your own burgers then."

Angus said two words that Joel didn't hear properly because of a big truck that went past. But judging by the angry look on his face and the second word sounding like 'you,' he could imagine what the first word was. The Irish Trio turned and left, and Joel knew from that moment, they were no longer his friends, but they were not a great loss.

He carried on to the shop where it all began. When he got there, he took one deep breath and walked in. He put his hand out to push open the door, but it opened automatically. The old door had been replaced by an electric one. The thought briefly flashed through his mind that he wouldn't have been caught if that electric door had been there a year ago.

He had butterflies as he entered. He wasn't sure what he was expecting to happen, but nothing did. It felt like an anticlimax. He made his way slowly up the first aisle and then walked down the second. As he got to the end, he saw Ivan entering the first aisle. As he watched him walk out of sight, he was surprised at how much Ivan seemed to have aged. He looked ten years older. He was also surprised to see him there. He thought Ivan had moved away.

He walked back up the first aisle. Ivan was stood with a can in his hand, reading the label.

"Ivan. How are you?"

Ivan looked up and immediately looked uncomfortable when he saw Joel. He nervously put the can back on the shelf.

"I'm fine. How are you?"

"I'm good now. Almost back to normal."

"That's great to hear. Listen, I'm sorry for all that happened, you know, closing the business, and, well, you being in hospital and everything. It was a dark time for me."

"Me too." There was an uncomfortable pause. "I thought you moved away. Are you back?"

"No. No I'm not back. I never moved away. I just moved across town. Speaking of which, I need to get back there. I'm glad you're okay now. See you."

Joel watched him walk back down the aisle and out the front door. He was walking quickly as though he couldn't get out of there fast enough. It was sad really, that in just one year Ivan had gone from being his friend, neighbour and boss, to someone who didn't want to speak to him and couldn't get away from him quick enough.

He sighed and turned to carry on up the aisle and saw Algar walking towards him.

"Joel, it's good to see you looking so well after the terrible year you've had."

Joel was puzzled wondering how Algar would know what sort of year he'd had.

"You remember me?"

"Of course. We had a talk that night and after that you lost your job and was hurt by your boss who lost his daughter. It was the only thing anyone talked about for months."

"Oh, that's how you know."

"Come out back with me. We'll talk."

"Wow. There's Déjà vu right there."

Algar laughed. "I promise it won't be like last time, unless you have a sandwich hidden up your sleeve."

It was Joel's turn to laugh. "Never again."

They walked through the store together and sat at the small table in the lunchroom which didn't look like it had changed since he was last there.

"So, you're still working here."

"Yes. I like it here so I have no reason to leave. What are you doing now?"

"Nothing yet. It's been a long road to recovery and in fact tonight is the first time I've been out alone and without a walking aid."

Algar smiled. "That's good news, and great that it happened exactly one year from when it all started."

"You know it's been exactly one year?"

"Of course. I marked it on the calendar. I mark down all incidents that happen here, but I took extra interest in yours as soon as it started a chain reaction which, as you recall, I did warn you about."

"Yeah, I remember, karma."

"That's correct. And I was more right than I wanted to be. I have to admit I never thought it would get so bad for you."

"Look, I know a lot of bad things happened after that, but it had nothing to do with what happened here."

"On the contrary. This is exactly where it all started, and it was all because of that one sandwich you destroyed."

Joel stared at him. There was no way that the sandwich theft caused Nadine to die. Algar said, "I saw you talking to Ivan tonight."

"You know Ivan?"

"Oh, yes. He used to be a regular customer. He was also here exactly one year ago too. He came in just after you left."

"That's just a coincidence. It had nothing to do with me."

"There's no such thing as a coincidence."

"That was definitely a coincidence. We weren't even in here at the same time."

"I know, but Ivan came in wanting a salad sandwich. There were none on the shelf, so he asked me if I had one out the back. I did, but it was the one you destroyed. If you hadn't, it would have been on the shelf and Ivan would have bought it."

"So what?"

"Well, Ivan chose another sandwich instead, Egg Mayonnaise."

"I still don't see the connection."

"While he was paying for it he said that his stomach felt a bit 'iffy' and so he wanted a quick sandwich instead of a full meal. The salad sandwich probably would have been okay, but the eggs, as sometimes happens, caused him to have diarrhea, which meant he couldn't drive his pregnant daughter home. And the rest, as we say, is history.

Joel was silent. He didn't know how to respond. After a few moments he said, "How do you know about the diarrhea?"

"His son-in-law Owen. He told a few people who told a few people. You know how it goes. Ivan blamed himself for a long time for eating an egg sandwich on an upset stomach. But no one could have predicted what would happen. Some people get constipated from eating eggs, others don't.

"What it comes down to is that we never know what's going to happen so we should always do the best we can so as not to invite bad karma into our lives."

"Invite? We don't ask for it to come into our lives. Why would we?"

"Not with words. Karma works through our actions. So, when we do bad things, especially when we know it's wrong, we're inviting bad karma. It can be a hard lesson to learn."

Joel was thoughtful for a minute. "I remember you saying that a hummingbird flapping its wings in America can cause a typhoon in Japan. I guess that night was something like that."

"Yes it was. But one thing you have to remember too, is that life is great at teaching us lessons. When bad things happen, even if we think we've hit rock bottom, what we have to remember is the only way is up. The ending of something old is the beginning of something new. If we let it."

"What about Ivan? He lost his daughter."

"He can make a fresh start. Grief is hard, but emotions don't last forever. Ivan eventually realised he needed a fresh start, even though he was troubled by his loss of a child and hurting you at the same time. He's not a stupid man. He can start over if he allows it. Time is a great healer."

"You make it sound so simple."

Oh no. It's not simple. Our emotions can be crippling. How about you? How did you cope during all the bad things that were happening to you?"

Joel thought for a few seconds, then smiled. "It was hard at first because it all seemed so unfair. I'd done nothing wrong, yet I'd lost my job and had an accident and was stuck in hospital for months.

"Luckily, there was this really cute girl who worked in the hospital gift shop and delivered gifts to patients. One day she delivered stuff to me, and that was it. We've been together ever since."

Algar smiled broadly. "That's wonderful. A new beginning at a time when you must have felt you'd hit rock bottom."

"Absolutely. I hadn't thought about it like that."

"Well, that's one thing that's worked out well for you. What about the financial side of it? Did you get a good payout for your injuries?"

"You mean, did I sue Ivan? No. It's funny, someone else asked me that not too long ago."

"Did you?"

"Why would I? It was an accident."

"That's what insurance is for. You don't sue him per se, you claim off his insurance. You've been incapacitated and unable to work for a year. They owe you money and a lot of it."

"I hadn't thought of that. But I don't know where he lives anymore."

"Get a lawyer. They can find anyone, and they can get you a bigger payout than you could get on your own. Do it tomorrow. Find a lawyer who specialises in compensation claims. You could end up quite wealthy."

Joel smiled. "I'm going to do it. I didn't want to pile any more grief onto Ivan, but I don't mind claiming from his insurance company. Thanks."

"You're welcome. But I'd better get back to work. I'm glad you came in tonight."

"Me too. I just felt like I had to come here tonight. I'm glad I did. Thanks again."

Joel walked back through the shop on his own. As he walked past the end of the aisles, he saw a familiar face. She was choosing a packet of chips and she turned as he stopped and looked at her.

For a moment they looked at each other in puzzlement, as though they were having the same thought.

He felt like he'd seen her in here before, in that exact same aisle, picking up a packet of chips.

Then he remembered. When he was in here a year ago and he and his friends were walking past the aisles, scoping out how many customers there were, and how they were going to grab sandwiches and run, he'd seen this same pretty, blonde girl in the same place.

When he saw her last year, she'd also looked back at him, and he'd briefly thought that at any other time, he'd have stopped and pretended he wanted chips too in order to strike up a conversation with her and ask her out.

He remembered thinking that there was just something about her that made him want to talk to her. It was more than how attractive she was. Somehow, when she'd looked up and smiled at him that day, he'd felt a connection to her.

She had felt the same one year ago when she'd stopped in to buy a packet of chips to eat. She was planning to watch a movie that night and wanted a snack to go with it.

Then she'd seen him. The cute guy with the wavy hair. He looked and smiled at her as he passed by the end of the aisle, and she'd smiled back and felt an instant connection with him. It was a feeling she couldn't explain, but it felt good and so real.

Unfortunately, he was with some other guys, and he disappeared with them. She'd bought her chips and left the shop without seeing him again.

And now, a year later, they were both here again. She was picking up a packet of chips and he was passing the end of the aisle. And just like before they smiled at each other. Only this time she understood the connection.

Why had she not seen it before? Why had she not recognised him? She certainly recognised him this time.

They walked towards each other, kissed and hugged.'

She said to him, "Oh my god, it's you. Do you remember seeing me here before?"

"Yeah, I do. I had no idea who you were or that I'd meet you again."

"Me neither," said Amelia. "Does this mean we met a year ago and didn't recognise each other when we met again at the hospital?"

Joel laughed. "I guess so. Maybe if we'd met in here again, we might have recognised each other."

Amelia was laughing too. "I can't believe this. I remember seeing you in here a few weeks before I saw you in hospital and I thought you were really cute. I had no idea the guy in the bed was the guy in the shop."

"I didn't recognise you again either. How weird is that? We met twice, fancied each other both times, yet didn't realise it was the same person."

"Well, at least we felt the same way both times we met so clearly it was meant to be. And look at you, here all alone and no stick."

"Yeah. I went shopping with Mum this afternoon without my stick and wanted to come out on my own tonight without it too."

"So, what brought you here?"

"I wanted to come back to where it all happened."

"Where what all happened?"

"Everything. Including meeting you, it seems. That is so weird that even we, us, started here."

"I still don't get it."

"I was in here exactly one year ago today and a chain of events happened." He saw Amelia's brow furrow. "It's a long story and I'm hungry. Want to get something to eat?"

"Sure." She put the packet of chips back on the shelf and they left the shop.

"Where are we going?" she asked him.

"Oh, I don't know. Let's just start walking and see where we end up. As long as we get there together, that's all that matters." He held her hand as they walked.

Amelia was touched. "You mean that?'

"You bet. You know, it feels as though we've always been together. In fact, it's hard to remember a time in my life without you in it. And I love that. I love that you've become such a big part of my life."

"Oh Joel," she said. "I feel the same way. You've become such a big part of my life too, and I can't imagine being without you. But sometimes I worry so much that as you get your life back, you won't want me in it anymore."

"I have to confess that sometimes I worried that you'd get bored with waiting for me to get better. I always wondered if you'd stay. But you did."

"So, you're better now and you still want me?"

"More than ever." He let go of her hand and put his arm around her as they walked. She slipped her arm around his waist. He carried on talking and she loved listening to him. "You know, my being better is a new beginning for us. It's not the end of something good, but the beginning of something great. Us."

Amelia couldn't speak. She was so happy she thought she might cry.

"Also, it turns out I may be rich too. Looks like I might be coming into money. The only way for me at the moment is up. Plus, I went on a radical diet tonight and lost around 250 unwanted kilos. All three of them. My life just keeps getting better."

Amelia started laughing. "I have absolutely no idea what you're talking about. But if it makes you happy, it makes me happy."

"Good. I'll explain it all over dinner. How about we get a takeaway and eat it in the park by the ocean. It's a special night, I'm with my special person and so I want to do our special thing."

She loved it that he called their picnics at the beach their special thing. She was happy that they had a special thing that they shared together. Their own private, special thing that no one else was invited to. Ever.

"I love our special thing."

"I love you," he said as he turned and kissed her.

She said, "I love you too."

Joel said, "I think I've loved you since the moment our eyes met a year ago."

Amelia thought that no words had ever sounded sweeter, until his next words when he said, "Come on. Let's go and enjoy the first day of the rest of our lives."

The End.